"YOU! GUNSLICK!" BELLOWED YOKUM. "GO FOR YOUR GUNS!"

The bar cleared instantly. Slowly, Dan turned to face the angry man. He lined his gaze on the dark, burning eyes.

"I said, go for your guns, hotshot! Got in a lucky punch, then stole me blind. You'll never do that again!"

"Holster that gun, mister," Dan said evenly. "I don't want to kill you."

Pete Lilly moved out of the line of fire. Dan saw the signal flash in Yokum's eyes. His draw was like the flitting tongue of a diamondback rattler. Both Colts belched fire. . . .

MORGAN HILL:
Bold Young Storyteller of the Old West

THE DAN COLT WESTERN SAGA:
Volume I: TWIN COLTS
Volume II: THE QUICK AND THE DEADLY
Volume III: BOOT HILL BROTHER
Volume IV: TEN MUST DIE
Volume V: BANDITS IN BLUE

Also by Morgan Hill:
DEAD MAN'S NOOSE

*Morgan Hill's Western novels
are published by Dell Books.
Ask your bookseller!*

BANDITS IN BLUE

Morgan Hill

A DELL BOOK

Published by
Dell Publishing Co., Inc.
1 Dag Hammarskjold Plaza
New York, New York 10017

Copyright © 1981 by Morgan Hill

All rights reserved. No part of this book may be reproduced or transmitted in any form or by any means, electronic or mechanical, including photocopying, recording or by any information storage and retrieval system, without the written permission of the Publisher, except where permitted by law.

Dell ® TM 681510, Dell Publishing, Co., Inc.

ISBN: 0-440-10421-1

Printed in the United States of America
First printing—December 1981

BANDITS IN BLUE

CHAPTER ONE

The first arrow hissed angrily just over his head. The second one splintered and caromed off the saddle horn, before Dan Colt had time to react.

He raked the big black gelding's sides savagely. The startled beast dug in and lunged forward, heading up the steep draw. Rocks scattered and tumbled behind the mighty hooves.

Yelping Comanches were galloping out of the heavily wooded thicket that straddled the narrow path. Whipping out his right-hand .45, the tall, blond man twisted in the saddle and snapped a shot at the lead Indian. As the gun roared, the bullet caught the pinto flush between the eyes. Blood spurted, followed by a deep grunting sound. The animal's legs gave way instantly, dumping its rider. The dead pinto, legs flailing, rolled down the precipitous slope toward the whooping bronze-skinned riders who followed.

The next pinto in line shied at the rolling horse,

spilling its rider. Horses were neighing in fear, eyes bulging. The barebacked Comanches were fighting to stay aboard their mounts.

The chaos caused in the restricted area between the rows of thick rabbit brush and abundant mesquite trees was enough to give Colt the head start that he needed. There was not a pinto alive that could catch the huge ebony-colored gelding.

As Dan topped the steep incline, he cast a backward glance. The furious Comanches were whipping their horses mercilessly, trying to force them against the protruding mesquite branches, and around the fallen horse.

The tall man gave the black its head. He could feel the power of the brute beneath him, eating up ground and loving it. The coal-black mane danced in the wind, as the man in the saddle threw another glance behind him. The Comanches still had not appeared. The flat land of New Mexico stretched out before horse and rider as they veered north and the high-spirited beast settled into a dead-heat run.

Off to the left, Dan could see the lazy Rio Grande as it wound its way south toward Las Cruces and El Paso. The waters were smooth, making the river look like a ribbon of glass in the early afternoon sun.

Dan Colt had been warned during his brief stop at Deming that the Comanches had painted up and were once again on the warpath. Apparently, as a lone rider approaching in a moment when they were deeply occupied, he had taken the Indians somewhat by surprise. Whatever they were doing back in the bush had been interrupted by the sound of the horse's hooves on the rocky terrain. Had they been lying in wait, the first arrow would not have missed.

As the wind whistled in his ears, Dan looked back again. The angry Comanches were bobbing over the top of the hill, one-by-one in single file. The black had given him a half-mile lead. The whooping Indians stayed with it until Dan had gained a full mile on them and it became evident that the spread between them was growing larger. They pulled rein in a cloud of dust and gave up the chase.

Seeing them fall behind, Dan wondered how many might be up ahead.

As soon as the Comanches were out of sight, Colt eased the black to a brisk trot and let him cool off slowly. The horse would not cool very much before sundown. The persistent August sun would see to that.

Doing a careful panorama, Dan studied the land for signs of more Indians. As he did so, he could not help but marvel at the singular beauty of this part of the country. Rich in various shades of brown and tan, the desert spread for miles in every direction. On the western horizon were the long plateaus, deep red on the sides of their jagged cliffs and luxuriously green along the horizontal levels at the top.

To the northeast stood the majestic Sandia Mountains, rough and irregular in formation, which added to their grandeur and beauty. Socorro lay sixty miles due north. Beyond that, some seventy-five miles, was Albuquerque.

There was a quiet peacefulness along the banks of the Rio Grande. Dan Colt had time to muse on his situation. The afternoon passed without incident.

Morgan Hill

As the desert sun touched the lush plateaus on the horizon, the waters of the river adopted the vibrant colors of the sunset. The world of powder and sand which flanked the broad stream lost its bleached look and took on a red hue.

Veering the big horse off the flats, Dan rode toward the river. Dismounting on the bank, he knelt down and drank upstream from where the gelding took his fill of water. The tall man removed his hat and splashed the cool liquid in his face.

Standing again to his full height of six feet five inches in his boots, Dan shaded his eyes against the lowering sun. He could make out the silhouette of the town of Williamsburg, nestled on the sand against the fire on the western horizon.

Swinging swiftly into the saddle, he said, "Well, boy, you'll have a nice bucket of oats for supper and I'll have me a steak."

It was almost dark as the blond man on the black horse reined in at the Williamsburg stable. Instructing the hostler to feed the gelding well and give him a good rubdown, Dan Colt threw the saddlebags over his shoulder and walked up the dusty street, following his nose. Passing the general run of bleached-out false-fronted frame buildings, he smelled hot food before he saw the sign. Squinting against the growing gloom, he eyed the faded lettering:

MAEBELL'S CAFE
GOOD FOOD—LOW PRICES

There was a steady hum of voices in the over-crowded eating place. As the tall man stepped

BANDITS IN BLUE

through the door, he could see that there was no place to sit. Every table and the seats at the counter were full. Two rowdy-looking cowboys, who were on their feet waiting for a seat, eyed him with scorn.

Flipping them a vagrant smile, Dan said, "Guess I'll come back later."

One said something to the other that Dan could not distinguish, as he stepped back on the street. The pattern of his life for nearly nine months, now, was to begin his search at the saloons and gambling places. The threshold of each place offered its own particular challenge. If Dave was in there, Dan must be fully prepared for whatever reaction came from the outlaw twin brother.

If Dave was *not* present, but had been there, there was usually someone he had infuriated before leaving. Because the twins were perfectly identical, that someone would take out his anger on Dan.

And then there was the constant danger of a sharp-eyed lawman. Or worse yet, a greedy bounty hunter. Dan Colt's twin brother, known as Dave Sundeen, was wanted in Texas for robbery. Posters bearing an artist's conception of his face were plentiful all over the West. There was a price on his head.

It was too easy for Dan to be mistaken for Dave. The bitter memory of five months in Yuma Territorial Prison hung like a black thick cloud in Dan Colt's mind. Having escaped Yuma, he set out on a do-or-die hunt for his twin.

The lawman who arrested Dan in Holbrook, Arizona, believing he was Dave Sundeen, was now a U.S. Marshal. Logan Tanner's main goal in life was to put Dan back in Yuma. Tanner had never accepted Colt's story of a twin brother.

It was too early to visit the saloons. Chances of getting a lead on Dave were better when the crowds were larger. Dan decided to check in at the hotel and return to the cafe after the rush was over. With proper sustenance in his stomach, he would pay a visit to the saloons.

Williamsburg had only one hotel, the Desert Flower. It wasn't much, but it beat sleeping on the ground with the little night creatures and the coyotes. Depositing the saddlebags on the bed, Dan washed his hands and face. He ran a comb through his thick blond locks. Slipping the twin Colts from their tied-down holsters, he spun the cylinders, checking the loads. His years as a gunhawk had taught him never to be careless about his guns. One slip could mean a one-way ticket to Boot Hill. Stretching out on the bed, he lay down for a brief rest.

Darkness had claimed Williamsburg when Dan Colt crossed the dusty street and once again entered Maebell's Cafe.

Only a handful of customers were in the place, as the tall, square-shouldered man ran his gaze across the room. Eyes touched him casually, but none showed any recognition. Two cowboys sat at the counter, smoking and drinking coffee. The other six occupants sat at tables, four at one and two at another.

A girl, possibly twenty or twenty-one, was cleaning one of the tables. She wore a cotton print dress. Dan noted that she was pretty, with dark brown eyes that matched the color of her shoulder-length hair. Her face

BANDITS IN BLUE

had a freshly scrubbed look, with natural rose in her cheeks.

The door to the kitchen swung open. A large, robust woman of fifty passed through, carrying a tray of clean cups and glasses. Placing the tray on the end of the counter, she eyed the girl calmly and said, "Put these on the shelf when you get a minute, Jeanie."

Jeanie was wiping the table with a wet cloth. "Okay," she said with a smile.

Dan assumed that the big woman was Maebell. Fixing his eye on a corner table, he sauntered toward it, stepping past the dark-haired girl. As she turned, acknowledging the presence of the tall man, Jeanie's eyes met Dan's. "Good evening, sir," she said, smiling pleasantly.

"Howdy," responded Colt, returning the smile.

No sooner had Dan slacked into a chair, than Jeanie approached with a menu and water. "I'll get you some coffee right away."

"That'd be great," said Dan, tilting the gray Stetson to the back of his blond head.

Momentarily, the girl returned from behind the counter with a cup in one hand and a steaming coffeepot in the other. Dan studied the menu as the hot liquid gurgled in the cup, tantalizing his nostrils with its fresh aroma.

Slipping a small pad and pencil from her dress pocket, Dan's waitress said, "Fried chicken's all gone, sir, and we're out of greens. It's been extra busy tonight."

"'S all right," he replied, looking into her pretty face. "I had my mouth all set for a big juicy steak, anyhow. You got taters and gravy?"

"Mmm-hmm," hummed Jeanie, scribbling hastily on the pad. "We have a little homemade bread left. Would you like some of that with butter?"

"Sounds scrumptious. How about the apple pie? Are you out of that?"

"We have a couple pieces left."

"I'll take one of 'em."

"How do you want your steak cooked?"

"Medium rare," said Dan with a furtive grin, "I don't want it to kick me when I stab it. I just want it to *moo* a little."

Jeanie wrinkled her nose and giggled. "I'll tell Maebell. She'll fix it just right."

Dan sipped his coffee while he waited for the meal. The foursome at the one table finished eating, paid their bill, and left. Jeanie filled Dan's coffee cup a second time. As she moved back behind the counter, the door opened and two grimy drifters came in. Their foul smell found its way to Dan's nostrils. The two cowboys at the counter eyed them with disdain. One was big. He stood at six feet and weighed about two hundred and fifty pounds. He had immense shoulders, with neck and arms to match. A gunbelt was slung under his overhanging belly. There was a mean look in his eye.

The other man was slight in stature, about five feet nine. The big gun on his slender hip looked out of place—like someone had hung it on the wrong man. Neither of them had shaved in several days.

The man and woman who sat at the other occupied table cast them a loathing look. Talking loudly and laughing hoarsely, the repugnant pair found their way to a table and, scraping chairs needlessly, sat down. One unoccupied table separated them from the tall man wearing the twin Colts.

As Jeanie approached the drifters' table, Dan let his line of sight wander to the large window that faced the street. It was some six feet in height and the same in width. Actually it was a series of small windowpanes, frilled around the edge with curtains that matched the tablecloths. People passed idly by.

Dan's attention was drawn toward the form of the waitress as she approached with a tray bearing his meal. Tension lined her face, as she removed the plates from the tray and spread them before him.

"Hey, girlie, we're ready to order!" bellowed the big drifter.

Instantly, Jeanie wheeled and pulled the pad and pencil from her pocket.

"What you havin', Pete?" asked the big man.

The smaller man looked at the girl and said, "I'll have the steak, with mashed potatoes and gravy—and corn."

Jeanie scribbled nervously.

"I'll have the fried chicken," the big one said loudly. "Bring me a whole chicken."

"Oh . . . I . . . uh . . . forgot to tell you we're out of chicken," said the girl.

"It's on the menu, girlie," snapped the drifter, "bring me chicken."

Dan was cutting his steak. He paused and set his gaze on the big smelly man.

"I—I'm sorry, sir. We're out of chicken. We had an extra busy night and—"

"*It's on the menu!*" roared the man. "*I want*

chicken!" His big fist slammed the table, bouncing the water glasses and coffee cups.

Jeanie jumped.

Dan Colt pushed back his chair, chewing his steak like a cud. Easing around the table, he approached the big man as Maebell watched from the kitchen door and the patrons observed with interest.

The drifter's eyes rolled upward as Dan towered over him. Coolly, the tall man said, "Your noise is interrupting my meal, mister."

The big man scowled.

Chewing some more and smacking his lips, Dan continued, "Besides that, you're not acting like a gentleman in the presence of the lady. Now, she said there's no more chicken. Order somethin' else."

The smaller man looked Dan up and down and said, "Sure, Hunk. Why don'tcha order a steak? Er ... uh ... maybe *two* if you're real hungry?"

"Shut up, Pete," snapped Hunk Yokum, eyeing the tied-down Colts. Looking at Jeanie and ignoring Dan, he said, "Bring me two big steaks, a bowl of mashed taters, and a big bowl of gravy."

Casually, Dan returned to his table. Hunk spoke to Pete Lilly loud enough for Dan to hear. "Just because he wears them tied-down hog-legs, he thinks he can order people around."

Pete threw a nervous glance at the tall man.

"Never saw one of them hotshot gunslicks who could fight his way out of a wet sack," persisted Hunk. "Take away their guns and the yellow stripe down their back shows up."

Dan eyed the man caustically and kept eating.

Jeanie delivered the two men their food, after

which she brought Dan his apple pie and more coffee. As she headed for the kitchen, Hunk reached out and grasped her wrist. The girl shied like a frightened deer and tried to pull away. The big man squeezed down hard.

"You're hurting me," complained Jeanie, her face twisted.

"Since I couldn't have no chicken, how about a little sugar for Hunk, girlie?" bellowed the thick-bodied man.

Once more the girl attempted to free her wrist, to no avail.

Dan Colt dropped his fork, anger welling up inside him. Inbred in his every fiber was a distinct aversion for any man who mistreated a woman. He found it impossible to tolerate. His boots thumped the floor as he moved toward the man.

"Let go of her," rasped Colt, his blue eyes frigid.

"Mind your own business, sonny," sliced Hunk.

Reaching for the arm that held Jeanie, Dan dug his fingers into Hunk's fleshy forearm. Immediately, the pain caused the big man to release the girl. He tried to jerk his arm loose, but Dan's grip was like a steel vise.

Hank cursed. "Leggo my arm!" he snarled.

Dan eyed the big bowl of steaming brown gravy on the table. Leaning over, his lifted it upward with his free hand. Quickly, he released Hunk's arm with the other hand, knocked his hat to the floor, and dumped the hot gravy over his head.

CHAPTER TWO

The big man roared in pain. Stiffening, he overturned the table on his partner. Jeanie retreated to the back of the counter, moving next to Maebell. The two cowboys at the counter stood up. The couple at the other table sat wide-eyed.

Hunk leaped to his feet, wiping gravy from his eyes, which were red with fury.

"The best thing for you is to pay the lady for your meal and quietly walk out of here," Dan said huskily.

"Yeah, let's go Hunk," said Pete apprehensively.

Hunk set himself and swung a haymaker at the tall man. The agile Colt dodged the punch and countered with two popping blows on the man's nose. Hunk blinked and shook his head. He lunged for Dan like a maddened bull.

The tall, muscular Colt sidestepped the charging man and cuffed him on the back of the neck. Hunk staggered, slamming into the counter. Maebell and Jeanie blinked and clung to each other.

Eyes wild, Hunk wheeled and charged again, catching Dan in the midsection. The two sprawled on the floor, scattering tables and chairs.

Quickly gaining their feet, fists flew. Dan took a hard right on the jaw and countered with a right cross of his own. Hunk swayed heavily and came on strong. His back was to the large window. Colt set himself. With his full weight behind it, he fired a pistonlike punch, catching the big man flush on the jaw.

Dan felt the impact all the way to his ankles. Hunk bounded back, crashed through the window, and landed on his back on the boardwalk. He was out cold.

Dan flashed a hard look at Pete, who stood by the door, craning his neck to see out the window. "He got any money on him?"

"Some, I s-suppose," stammered Pete.

Turning toward Maebell, Colt said, "Looks like we busted a couple of chairs and a table, too, ma'am. How much you suppose the window and all this will cost to repair?"

The big woman stood with her arm around Jeanie. "I reckon about fifty-sixty dollars, stranger," she said nervously.

Swinging his glance back to Pete, Dan said, "See how much he's got on him."

The small man shook his head. "Please, mister. He'll kill me if I take his money. Don't make me do it."

Dan sighed disgustedly and stepped through the broken window. Ransacking Hunk's pocket, he found seventy-three dollars. Turning and looking through the window past the broken shards that clung to the edges, he said, "How much was his meal, ma'am?"

"Dollar and a half," responded Maebell.

People were gathering around the front of the cafe, staring at the unconscious man lying on the boardwalk, sprawled over the broken glass.

"How much was the little fella's meal?" Colt asked the big woman.

"Eighty cents."

Stepping back through the window, he palmed the seventy-three dollars on the counter. "This ought to cover the whole bill, plus a generous tip for the waitress." Turning to Pete, Dan said, "You just had supper on your friend, Pete. Now get him out of here."

"B-but I—"

"You what?"

"I didn't get to *eat* the meal," complained the little man.

Dan scowled. "Chalk it up to runnin' with the wrong company."

Hunk was beginning to stir, rolling his head on the broken glass.

"Go on," said Colt. "Get your partner on his feet and clear out."

Wordlessly, Pete moved through the door, elbowed his way past the crowd, and turned his efforts on the big man. Dan returned to his table, sat down, and went to work on the apple pie. Promptly, Jeanie appeared with the coffeepot. "Let me warm your coffee, Mister—"

"Colt, little lady," he said softly. "Dan Colt."

"I'm Jean Howard," she smiled. "Thank you for what you did."

Dan eyed the purple marks on the girl's wrist. "Looks like I should have stepped in a little sooner," he said apologetically.

Maebell stepped up beside the waitress. "Thank you, stranger," she said heartily. "Sure appreciate your helpin' Jeanie."

"My pleasure," said Dan around a chunk of apple pie. "Grinds my gizzard to see a man bully a woman."

Abruptly, a tall, lean man with a star on his vest came through the door. "What happened, Maebell?" he asked.

"Big dude got fresh with Jeanie, marshal," replied the woman, "but this here feller put him in his place."

"Who's paying for the window?" asked the lawman, studying the mess.

"It's all taken care of," said Maebell.

Jeanie spoke up. "Marshal Wren, this is Mister Dan Colt. Mister Colt, this is Doyle Wren, our town marshal."

Dan stood up and offered the lawman his hand. He hoped Wren did not have one of Dave Sundeen's wanted posters. "My pleasure, marshal," said Colt with a smile.

Wren blinked, looking hard at the blond man's face. Dan's heart froze. The handshake seemed to last an hour. The marshal spoke, "Not *the* Dan Colt. The gunfighter?"

Releasing Wren's hand, Dan felt a wave of relief. "Yeah. I'm him."

"But I heard you were ambushed somewhere up in Kansas and dropped in an unmarked grave."

"Just scuttlebutt, sir," said Colt. "I hung up my guns and took up ranching. Wyoming."

Wren glanced at the twin Colts. "Looks like you unhung 'em."

"Long story," responded Dan kindly, but in a tone that told Williamsburg's marshal that he was not going to hear the story.

Swinging his head back and forth, Wren said, "Where'd the culprit go?"

"Out that window," chuckled Maebell.

"But he paid you for the damage, huh?"

"Shore did, marshal," replied the rotund woman, chuckling again.

"All right," said Wren. "Guess my services aren't needed here. Good night." He started for the door. Stopping suddenly, he turned and looked at Dan, who was draining his cup. "Mister Colt . . ."

"Yes, marshal," Dan said, lowering his cup.

"Are you really as fast with them guns as people say?"

Raising his shoulders, the blond man said, "I don't know. I never drew against me."

The marshal smiled. "No, I guess not." With that, he left. The haunting thought which Dan Colt had lived with for nearly a year leaped into his mind. Dave Sundeen had a reputation for being fast. Mighty fast. *Would Dan have to draw against his twin? Which one was fastest? Could he kill his own brother?*

Dan shook his head, as if to throw the repugnant thoughts from his brain. Standing up, he said, "That was a fine meal, ladies." Reaching in his pocket, he pulled out a small wad of bills.

"Oh no you don't," objected Maebell. "Supper's on the house."

Dan started to protest.

Placing her palm on Colt's hand, Maebell said, "Please."

Tilting his well-formed head, Dan said, "Okay. Thank you, ma'am."

"Thank *you*," said Jeanie Howard.

Dan made his way up the street toward the first saloon. The town only had two, the Wrangler and the Red Rose. He doubted that there would be any word on Dave in this town. One thing for sure: The marshal had not seen him.

Dan could leave no stone unturned. He must check the saloons.

First appeared the Wrangler. The tall man's spurs jingled as he mounted the wooden sidewalk from the dusty street. The usual saloon sounds met his ears as he parted the batwings. A painted woman stood beside an upright piano, singing an old ballad. No one was paying her any particular attention. Voices comingled in the smoke-filled room, broken periodically by the outburst of hoarse laughter. The smell of smoke, whiskey, and cowboys was pungent.

The saloon was fully occupied, except for a couple of spaces at the bar. Moving into the first one, Dan glanced at the bartender, who was busy at the other end of the bar. Biding his time until he could get the man's attention, he turned slowly, exposing his face to the crowd. Vigilantly, he studied expressions as eyes met his from time to time. There was no sign of recognition.

Presently, a thick voice from behind him said, "What's yours, big fella?"

Turning quickly, Dan met the bartender's gaze. He was a large, bald man with a broad nose and heavy lips. "Just some information," smiled Dan. "You seen an *hombre* in here within the last few days looks like me?"

"Nope," the bartender answered quickly.

"You sure?" pressed Colt. "My brother. I'm needin' to find him."

"Never forget a face, mister," said the bald man. "If he looks anything like you, I ain't seen him." The bartender looked at the man leaning on the bar who stood to Dan's right. "Fred, you seen an *hombre* around who looks like him?"

The man emptied a shot glass and squinted at Colt. "Nope," he said, head bobbing. "But then, I don't shee too good 'bout half the time, ennyway."

"Thanks, just the same," said Dan, smiling at the bartender. Turning, he left the smoke and noise for the quietness of the street and the fresh night air. Angling across the dark street, he made for the Red Rose. Pushing his way through the creaking batwings, he found the same sounds and smells he had just left.

The bar was tightly packed. Dan's eyes roamed around the room. Dave's game was poker. If he had been in Williamsburg, he would have played poker. Threading his way among the tables, he found a poker game in progress. Stopping beside the table, he eyed the four cowboys. None of them noticed his presence.

BANDITS IN BLUE

"Could I bother you gentlemen for just a moment?" the tall man asked politely.

One man tossed him a sour glance.

Ignoring Dan's question, another threw some money in the pot and said, "I'll raise ya twenty."

"Excuse me," interjected Colt. "Could I ask a quick question?"

The cowboy who had just dropped the money eyed him with scorn and said, "What is it?"

"Have any of you seen a man looks like me in town lately?"

The four eyed Dan's angular face, looked at each other, and shook their heads. As they resumed the game, Colt stopped five others with the same results.

Making his way to the bar, he slipped in as one man stepped away. The bartender, a tall man with a heavily lined face said, "Whiskey, stranger?"

"Information," said Dan, smiling. "You seen a man looks like me? He'da been in here within the last few days."

"Sure ain't," replied the bartender.

Suddenly, the man standing to Dan's left said loudly, "Well, I'll be a suck-egg mule! If it ain't Dave Sundeen!"

Dan fixed his eyes on the man's face. It was vaguely familiar. "Do I know you?" asked Dan, surprised.

"Now, come on, Dave. You haven't forgotten already!"

Why was this man's face familiar? If Dave Sundeen knew him, certainly Dan Colt would not. Dan searched his brain.

The man squeezed Dan's right arm just above the elbow. "Still just as strong, I bet," he said smiling.

"Friend, I'm trying to place you, but—"

"Tommy Tompkins," he said shaking Dan's arm. "You know . . . *Yuma*! We busted rock together!"

Suddenly, Dan remembered the face. It had been much thinner at the prison. "Oh, sure, sure!" said Dan, shaking Tompkins's hand. "You look a little different with some flesh on your body."

"If you thought I looked bad when you saw me, you shoulda seen me when the cholera got through with me." Casting his eyes in both directions, Tompkins lowered his voice. "Only you had escaped by then."

"Yeah," Dan nodded, looking around to see if anyone was listening.

"They really talked about you around the prison, Dave. Your mysterious escape, I mean."

"When did you get out?" asked Dan, trying to divert the conversation from himself. All he needed was for word of this to leak to Doyle Wren and Dan would find himself behind bars again. He was trying to think of a way to shed himself of Tompkins, who was explaining his release from Yuma, when the batwings burst open with a loud bang.

It was Hunk Yokum. The big man had a purple mark on his jaw. In his hand was a .44 revolver. The hammer was thumbed back. He glowered savagely at Dan Colt, his face a florid mask of fury. Behind him, in the doorway, stood Pete Lilly, fear riding his countenance.

"You! Gunslick!" bellowed Yokum. "Go for your guns!"

Men scattered from the bar. One of the saloon girls ejected a whimper. Slowly, Dan turned to face the angry man. He lined his gaze on the dark, burning eyes. Colt had learned long ago that a man's eyes are the windows of his soul. Unless he has worked on camouflaging it, he will give a signal with his eyes before he draws. Or in this case, before he pulls the trigger.

Yokum would not be the first man to hold a gun on Dan Colt and end up dead on the spot. Dan had no desire to kill him, but if Yokum flashed a signal...

"I said, go for your guns, hotshot!" Hunk thundered again. "Got in a lucky punch, then stole me blind. You'll never do that again!"

"Holster the gun, mister," Dan breathed heavily in the silence that had fallen. "I don't want to kill you." His eyes never left those of Hunk Yokum.

Pete Lilly moved out of the line of fire.

Dan saw the signal flash in Yokum's eyes. His draw was like the flitting tongue of a diamondback rattler. Both Colts belched fire. One slug exploded Yokum's heart, while the other one centered his forehead. The big man's gun discharged, sending the bullet past Dan into one of the wooden beams that supported the roof. Yokum was slammed into the batwing doors by the double impact. He hit the board sidewalk with a sodden thud. The batwings clattered and squeaked.

Eyeing the onlookers, Dan said, "You all saw it. I had no choice. Be sure to tell the marshal." Tommy Tompkins stared in wonder at Colt's broad back as he holstered the guns and disappeared into the night.

CHAPTER THREE

Five miles due north of Williamsburg, Colonel Jeffrey Allen was camped on the east bank of the Rio Grande with a platoon of twenty cavalrymen.

The colonel had been dispatched from Fort Denning, just north of Las Cruces, to take charge of Fort Ryan, which lay some twelve miles south of Socorro. The Comanches were plundering and killing all over the area. The general at El Paso had put Allen in charge of Fort Ryan. His experience in Indian fighting was needed in this central location.

The platoon, led by Lieutenant Richard Puter, had journeyed from Fort Ryan to escort the colonel to his new place of duty. The detachment actually had a dual purpose. Eight thousand dollars of army payroll money was being transported inconspicuously in the saddlebags of Corporal Tim Baker. Half was for the payroll at Fort Ryan. The other half was to be delivered to the paymaster at Fort Lewis, near Durango,

BANDITS IN BLUE

Colorado. Each half represented a full year's pay for both forts.

Unbeknownst to Colonel Allen and Lieutenant Puter, a group of dissidents had formed within the ranks of the platoon. Sergeant Joe Caraway was the virulent leader of the pack. He and his nine followers had agreed to desert the army and its low pay. They would travel the West on a robbing spree, wearing their blue uniforms. Vulnerable people, thinking they were legitimate cavalrymen, would be caught off guard and become easy prey. Their masquerade would be short-lived. They must work fast. Word would spread like wildfire.

As three campfires burned against the darkness of the warm August night, the unscrupulous Caraway maneuvered his men into a casual group. Hoping to appear inconspicuous, he wanted to give last-minute instructions for tomorrow's aggressive move.

While Colonel Allen and Lieutenant Puter conversed with the other men, Caraway said in a heavy whisper, "Coupla you fellas talk loud . . . laugh a little. Make it sound normal. I'll explain things to the rest. They can fill you in."

Private Ken Deere and Private Lester Worth immediately struck up a loud conversation.

"We'll do it when we stop to water the horses the first time," said Caraway. "Puter will call for it somewhere between two and three hours after we pull out. When the horses are drinkin', the ten of us will walk our mounts out into the river. Very casually." Caraway kept his voice at a whisper. From time to time, he shot a glance at the other group, which seemed engrossed in conversation.

A coyote howled nearby.

"When you hear me holler at the colonel to look behind him, start shootin'," continued Caraway. "We gotta kill 'em all. We'll have a lot longer to rob banks and stagecoaches if the colonel and the rest of 'em are dead. We'll bury them and scatter the horses. We'll rob the bank at Socorro first . . . and head north."

The slender sergeant lifted his hat, ran his fingers through his blond hair, and said, "Stevens, you concentrate on Baker, as I told you before. Don't fail to grab his horse. We'll divvy up the eight thousand after we bury the dead."

"Will do," agreed Private Frank Stevens.

"Do we have to *kill* 'em?" put in Corporal Lon Ward. Light from the fire revealed a worried look on his young face. "Couldn't we just tie 'em up good and head out?"

Caraway's countenance was marked by dark shadows. His eyes formed into small black beads. His subdued voice was cynical. "You got chicken feathers for guts, Ward?"

Ward blinked nervously. "No. I just don't like murder."

Tight-lipped, Caraway said, "You knew the plan before we left Fort Ryan, Ward. You agreed that army life stinks. You said you wanted in on this." The malevolent eyes of the lantern-jawed sergeant lay hard on Corporal Lon Ward. "Now, you're *in*, mister. And Allen, Puter and the rest of 'em all die. Understand?"

Ward bit his lower lip and nodded wordlessly. Caraway fixed his eyes on Ward for a long moment. In fear, the young corporal held his gaze.

Looking again at the others, Sergeant Caraway said, "I'm movin' on now. Don't want Puter to get suspicious. You boys make sure Deere and Worth understand. Each one of you has been assigned his own man to kill. As I told you before, I'll handle Puter and Allen. Use your revolvers. The instant I call to Allen to look behind him . . . *draw and cut 'em down.*"

Lieutenant Richard Puter was a muscular man in his early thirties. Standing three inches under six feet, he wore a heavy black moustache, which matched the fringe of hair at the base of his otherwise bald head. Perceptive and experienced in handling men, he sensed an uneasiness growing within him toward Sergeant Joe Caraway.

As Puter stood by the fire listening to Colonel Allen discuss the Comanche problem, he threw a casual glance toward the group that had gathered with Caraway. The inward uneasiness pressed tight against his spine.

The lieutenant contemplated the wisdom of mentioning his suspicions to Colonel Allen. There was nothing tangible to go on. Just a look in Caraway's eyes the past several weeks. Conversations cut short on his approach to the sergeant and a select few men, but no conclusive evidence of anything.

Puter had seen men desert the army before. The pressures of Indian warfare in a raw and foreboding land often built up within men. This, coupled with meager pay and long periods away from wives and sweethearts, sometimes pushed a man beyond his limits. This became especially dangerous when the dissidence against the army was born in the heart of a man with rank—especially a man like Joe Caraway. There was in the tall, yellow-haired sergeant, a mean streak, which was both feared and admired by the other men. Caraway was a leader. In the wrong frame of mind he could be a dangerous man.

Puter had watched Caraway in Indian battles. The sergeant enjoyed killing. Many a red man had been dipped in the sod because his lot fell to face the yellow-haired man in mortal combat. One thing for sure: Joe Caraway was no coward. If he ever deserted, it would be because of greed or discontent. Never for fear of battle.

The lieutenant wrestled with the prodding instinct that picked at his spine like barbed wire. As he saw Caraway detach himself from the group and move in his direction, Puter decided to observe the sergeant a little longer. If only there was more evidence . . .

As Caraway drew near, he spoke to Puter, "Lieutenant, I'll choose three men and take the first watch, if it's all right with you."

"Sure, Sergeant," responded Puter. "Go ahead and assign each watch."

The tall sergeant wheeled and walked away.

Puter agreed with the colonel, who remarked that the men should bed down for the night. As they scattered to do so, he casually strolled toward Corporal Baker, who was easing his saddlebags to the ground at a spot where he had chosen to sleep. Softly, he said, "Tim, I'll bed down beside you. When I flop my saddle and bags to the ground, I want you to switch the bags. I'll put the money on my horse in the morning."

BANDITS IN BLUE

Baker eyed the lieutenant warily. "You know something I don't?" he whispered.

"Not really. Just a feeling I have."

"Sure, lieutenant. Whatever you say. We're far enough from the fire. Nobody will notice."

Corporal Lon Ward was assigned to the fourth watch. He was admonished by Sergeant Caraway to get right to sleep. As he lay, head on saddle, however, sleep eluded him. There was a knot rolling in his stomach like a hot rock. How had he ever gotten mixed up with Caraway, anyhow? It was not an intentional thing. He had joined the army four years previously at Fort Banner, Texas. Things had been dull there. Two years had passed and he hadn't even fired a gun, except in target practice. The whole idea behind his enlistment was the adventure and action of army life.

Then came word of Indian trouble in New Mexico and Colorado. The army needed men to train as cavalry troopers. Three months after volunteering, Lon Ward climbed into a blue uniform with cavalry-yellow stripes on the trouser legs and silver buttons on the coat. He donned the gray hat that bore crossed sabers on its crown and strapped the silver saber on his waist.

Life on horseback came naturally. A sharp eye for army particulars and a keen sense of duty put the two chevrons on his sleeve in record time. He was the only corporal under twenty-three. Lon Ward found that he possessed fortitude for battle. He was a good trooper. The cavalry would be his career.

Then came the letters.

First was the one from his mother. Bobby, his

older brother, had gone into business with Mr. Parker, the owner of Amarillo's dry goods store. He was earning ninety-five dollars a month and within a couple of years would be a full-fledged partner. This marred Lon's ego. Bobby was big stuff in Dad's eyes, too. The army's eleven dollars a month looked a little puny alongside Bobby's earnings.

Then came the letter from Annie Sue. She had made him a promise on that warm summer night on her front porch. She loved him, she said . . . and would wait for him. The letter revealed that Annie Sue had married Homer Stanford. Homer had taken special training and now was employed in the local abstract office. He was making more money already than a *captain* makes in the army.

Joe Caraway happened to voice his displeasure with army pay to Ward the same day Annie Sue's letter arrived. Feeling a sudden resentment toward the U.S. government, Lon was open prey for Caraway's idea of desertion. Then came word of the trip to Las Cruces. *Eight thousand dollars!*

Caraway already had eight men lined up. If he could get one more, it would be even, except for the colonel. With the element of surprise on their side, Caraway and his ten men could wipe out eleven without too much trouble.

The eight thousand would be divided equally. Lon Ward did a little quick arithmetic. He would have eight hundred dollars. At corporal's pay, it would take him *six years* to make that much money! And that would only be the beginning. Leaving Puter, Allen, and the rest of the troopers dead, it would take the army awhile to figure things out. In the meantime, they could ride north and have a bandit's holiday.

Now, on the eve of the insurrection, there was one part of all this that galled Ward's stomach: *leaving Puter, Allen, and the rest of the troopers dead.* But it was too late to change the situation. Ward could double-cross Caraway and inform Lieutenant Puter of the diabolical plan. However, this would be no insurance that Caraway would not find a way to kill Ward.

No, Corporal Lon Ward was like a man on a runaway train down a mountainside. He had no choice. He would have to ride it all the way. The thought of facing his conscience over the bloodshed plagued him. Maybe the money would help ease his conscience. At least it sounded good right now.

Dawn came with a rose flush on the eastern rim of the earth.

Corporal Lon Ward had not slept. He had remained wide awake through the fourth watch.

After a breakfast of coffee and military rations, the platoon made ready to travel. Lieutenant Richard Puter laid the black McClellan saddle on his horse's back and cinched it down tight. Carefully, he buckled the saddlebags to the saddle and watched Tim Baker do the same with the other ones. The two men eyed each other furtively.

Approaching the colonel, Puter said, "We're ready to move out, sir."

Allen ran his fingertips through his dense gray moustache. "All right, Puter, let's do it."

Richard Puter swung into the saddle, guided his mount to the head of the column, and turned in the saddle. Sergeant Caraway was conversing quietly with the man next to him. Puter had the same sensation along the ridge of his backbone that he had felt the night before.

Again, there was the urge to reveal it to the colonel. But . . . what if he was wrong? Even if he was right, how could he prove it?

Thoughts were racing through his brain. *At least, I could warn Allen. We would be somewhat prepared.* Then the thought struck him that if an act of rebellion was in the making, which men were in on it for sure? There was no way to know. He would stay alert himself. There was one slight touch of comfort. They didn't know he and Baker had switched saddlebags.

The Rio Grande flowed quietly on the left flank of the platoon as Lieutenant Richard Puter raised his right hand, thrust it ahead, and bellowed, "Forward, ho!"

The column moved out with the sound of tinkling metal and squeaking saddles. Two or three horses blew and they were under way. The desert sun touched them on the right, with the promise of heat.

The land was rugged, broken with gullies and dry washes. There was green grass for two hundred yards on each side of the river. At that point, the grass quickly faded to a dull yellow, finally merging into desolate acres of scrub brush and sand. From time to time, there were marshy pockets along the riverbank where clusters of willow trees stood. Closer to the mountains to the east and west black chaparral grew with dotted patches of mesquite.

Riding next to the lieutenant, Colonel Jeffrey Allen slitted his eyes against the growing glare. "They could hit us any time," spoke up Allen.

Puter, with his mind on the ignominious misgiving that picked at his spine, looked wide-eyed at the colonel. "What did you say, sir?"

"I said they could hit us any time."

Slightly stunned, Puter said, "Who, sir?"

"The Comanches, lieutenant," retorted Allen. "Who did you think I meant?"

"Sorry, colonel," he said apologetically. "Guess I was daydreaming."

Viewing the terrain, the experienced eye of the silver-haired colonel tried to anticipate the place where the Comanches might spring an ambush. Indians were like prairie dogs. They seemed to blend into the land.

When they attacked in this desert country, there was little warning.

Colonel Jeffrey Allen was a big man. Standing six feet two, he weighed over two hundred and thirty pounds. Although in his early sixties, he was stalwart and tough. His face was leathered and tanned. The gray in his moustache and full head of hair served to add a touch of dignity to his rugged features.

Allen had fought in the Civil War. On the Union side, he had killed many a rebel on the battlefields in Virginia, Kentucky, and Tennessee. Since coming to the West, he had engaged in a number of Indian battles, even as a colonel. He once kept track of the red men he had sent into eternity. When the number reached over a hundred, he scrapped the idea. Only one man out of the great number he had killed wore a blue uniform. *A deserter.* The man had turned tail in battle and run away. Within three hours, Allen had caught him and killed him with his bare hands. The colonel hated a deserter more than a rattlesnake. More than a bloodthirsty Comanche.

CHAPTER FOUR

Two hours passed. The temperature continued to rise. Joe Caraway eyed the glistening river. He wondered how soon the lieutenant would give the command to halt and break rank to water the horses.

A mounting dread was moving through Corporal Lon Ward's system like cold molasses. He hoped Puter would delay the stop a little longer. A rivulet of sweat ran down his back.

Another hour passed. The sun hung in the brassy sky, a menacing ball of torment.

Lieutenant Richard Puter took a long drink from his canteen and thought of the thirsty horses. Running his gaze along the bank of the Rio Grande as it wended its way northward, he saw a shallow valley ahead. There was a low spot where the bank was almost level with the water. A few willows offered a bit of shade.

Twisting in the saddle, Puter spoke to Sergeant

Caraway, who rode directly behind him, "Sergeant, pass the word. We'll stop for water in the bottom of that valley up ahead."

Caraway's pulse quickened. A dry smile parted his lips. He quickly relayed the message to the troopers just behind him.

A trace of concern lined the face of Colonel Allen. There were hills and gullies on both sides of the river in the valley. Comanches could be hiding among them, ready to attack. Lifting his eyes upward, the colonel pondered the crest of the rise on the other side of the valley.

When word reached the ears of Lon Ward, a hot feeling spread in his stomach. A wave of nausea washed over him. He wanted to spur his horse and run away. His heart was pounding. He could feel the throb of the pulse in his temples.

With a firm tone in his voice, the colonel spoke to Puter. "Lieutenant, I think it unwise to take our water in that spot."

"Sir?" responded Puter.

"If the Comanches would come out of those low places or from behind those hills, we'd have nowhere to take cover."

"Whatever you say, sir." Puter smiled. "You've been at this Indian fighting longer than I have."

"Let's wait till we get over the ridge on the other side of the valley. I believe we'll find a safer place."

"Yes, sir." The broad-shouldered lieutenant turned in the saddle, looking Caraway in the eye. "Colonel Allen says we should wait till we get out of the valley. Not enough cover. Pass it on."

A touch of disappointment went through the sergeant. He was eager to get the thing done. He was already thinking that Puter couldn't have picked a better spot. Walking the horses into the river from a low bank would make the victims point-blank targets. If the bank was higher, they would be shooting at an angle. Reluctantly, he turned and informed the riders behind.

Lon Ward breathed a sigh when the message reached his ears. He was glad to pass it on.

The horses were showing strain when the column left the valley and topped the rise. Immediately, at the bottom of a long slope, Allen spotted a curve in the river which was fortressed on the east bank with several giant boulders. Standing ten to twelve feet high, they would afford safety in an attack. Pointing at the spot, the colonel spoke to Puter. "We'll stop by those boulders at the bend in the river, lieutenant. Send a couple men ahead to check it out. Make sure there are no Comanches hiding in them."

"Yes, sir," said Puter. Twisting in the saddle, he called, "Private Deere! Private Worth!"

Ken Deere and Lester Worth broke from the ranks and trotted to Puter's side.

"Yes, sir?" said Deere.

"You two ride ahead and check out those boulders at the bend in the river. We want to stop for rest and water there."

"Yes, sir," said Deere.

As the two privates galloped ahead, Joe Caraway turned casually in the saddle and glanced at Lon Ward. The corporal's face was pale. There was a hard look in Caraway's eye. The sergeant squared himself in the saddle. Ward stared at his sweat-soaked back.

Lon Ward was wishing he had never left Texas.

Officers Allen and Puter kept steady eyes on the two riders as they approached the boulders, drew their revolvers, and rode cautiously around them. For a moment Deere and Worth were out of sight. Presently, they appeared riding in the river, rounding the rock formation. Ken Deere waved the signal that all was well.

As Deere rode his mount out of the river onto the gentle slope of the bank, he spoke to Worth. "This spot is okay, if we kill 'em all with the first volley. If any of 'em get up into those rocks, they'll be hard to flush out."

"Shouldn't be any problem, if every one of us takes out his assigned man," said Lester Worth.

"Caraway has two to kill—both officers," said Deere worriedly.

"Don't fret about Joe. He will."

The column arrived where Deere and Worth sat their horses. The waters gurgled at the base of the boulders. Joe Caraway did a quick survey of the river bank. It was low enough to water the horses without riding into the river. He hoped his victims would do just that.

Lieutenant Richard Puter's voice bellowed through the hot desert air, "Column . . . halt!"

In a cloud of dust the cavalry platoon reined to a stop. "All right, men," said Puter, "dismount and water your horses."

Swerving toward the bank, Caraway said, "Some of

us will ride into the river and water there, sir. That way we can keep an eye on your flank."

Before Puter had acknowledged Caraway's offer, nine horses were splashing in the knee-deep water. Lon Ward felt like his chest was on fire. His whole body shook. As he drew rein and hesitated, Caraway bolted him with a hard stare.

Deep inside, Ward knew he could not go through with it. He could not murder a man in cold blood. Killing Indians in battle was one thing, but murder was something else.

Joe Caraway sensed it coming a split second before Ward shouted. He unsnapped the flap on his holster, just as Ward's words pierced the air, "Colonel! Lieutenant! They're gonna kill you!"

One moment the river bend was serene and calm. The next moment it was booming guns, screaming horses, shouting men—and running blood.

Raw fury ignited Joe Caraway's brain. Whipping the revolver from the holster, he fired point blank at Lon Ward, then swung the muzzle on the colonel and fired again.

Caraway's men, being caught off guard, were slow in drawing their weapons. The others almost matched them, gun for gun. The deserters had another edge, however. Each man knew just whom to shoot. For several seconds, Puter's men were confused.

When Caraway's slug tore into Ward's chest, he stiffened in the saddle, seemed to hang there a moment in the hot morning air, then peeled over the horse's side. Twisting as he fell, Ward's foot caught in the stirrup. The frightened animal lunged into the river, submerging the young corporal. As it bounded up the bank on the opposite side, his head split open on a large rock. The horse charged across the level ground at a full gallop. Lon Ward's body trailed, flopping like a rag doll.

Caraway's second shot was not as deadly. The slug ripped through Colonel Jeffrey Allen's left shoulder, toppling him from the horse. The wayward sergeant lost Lieutenant Puter in the gunsmoke of the first volley.

Puter had leaped from his saddle, drawing his gun. His .44 stabbed flame into the cluster of uniformed men who had spun their mounts in the river. One of the deserters Puter shot at screamed and fell in the river, his blood turning the Rio Grande a deep red.

As Puter snapped off another shot, he saw the colonel bounce on the ground, clutching his shoulder. The rugged, silver-haired man pulled his gun from its holster with his left hand and rolled up to one knee. He got off two rounds and fell over. Quickly, Richard Puter dashed to him, hoisting him upward. "Let's get into the rocks, colonel!" he shouted above the din.

Supported by the muscular officer's powerful arms, Allen soon found himself elevated about six feet off the ground between two boulders. The revolver was still in his left hand. Blood oozed through his fingers where he gripped his wounded shoulder.

When the shooting started, Frank Stevens took careful aim at Corporal Tim Baker and shot him dead. In the confusion of the moment, Stevens leaped from his saddle, stepped over the body of Baker, and mounted the dead man's horse.

Acrid blue smoke hung like fog in the air as guns continued to roar. Men were dropping like quail in a brush shoot. One of Puter's men headed for the safety of the giant boulders, when a bullet entered his back. The trooper straightened, staggered, and flopped face forward.

Richard Puter snapped a shot at the blue-uniformed deserter who had just killed the trooper. The man pitched headlong from his horse and hit the ground with a loud pop.

As men fought and died, the staccato of the gunfire echoed across the land, carrying over the hill and into the valley through which the column had just passed.

Dan Colt had ridden fast out of Williamsburg after killing Hunk Yokum. Any confrontation with the marshal could lead to his being mistaken for Dave Sundeen. He doubted that there would be a posse on his trail, because eyewitnesses would tell the marshal that Yokum invoked the gunfight.

Riding in the dark, Dan found a secluded spot about three miles north of Williamsburg. There, he took his rest for the night.

Rising at dawn, the tall man ate some beef jerky, drank from the Rio Grande, and hit the trail. About the time the sun lifted its fiery rim over the horizon, Dan spotted the tracks of the cavalry platoon. They veered up from the campsite on the river bank and pressed the grass that grew along the trail. There was no way to tell how many men were traveling in the column. Too many tracks. One thing for sure, they were not far ahead.

The morning wore on. The wary Colt kept a watchful eye for Indians. The sun grew hotter.

Dan had experienced a touch of disappointment in

learning that Dave had not been in Williamsburg. His course had been a straight line north out of Deming. Williamsburg would have been a natural stop for a traveler going this route. A note of fear rang in Dan's heart. What if Dave had suddenly taken another direction? He shook his head, as if to throw out the thought. No, Dave was still heading north. He had simply bypassed Williamsburg.

As the big black gelding carried Dan to the rim of a shallow valley, he spotted the column of troopers. They were just reaching the ridge on the opposite side of the valley. Quickly, Colt's keen eye counted twenty-one riders. Soon they disappeared over the ridge.

A giant hawk lifted itself from a stand of willow trees at the bottom of the valley, next to the river.

Lifting the canteen from the pommel, Dan took a long drink. The black nickered. "Okay, pardner," he said. "Let's get you a drink." Swinging off the trail and descending the gentle slope to the river, the tall man dismounted and let the animal take his fill. Kneeling on the bank, Dan removed his hat and splashed water in his face. Cupping his hands, he dumped the cool liquid on his head. Scanning the land for Indians and seeing none, he mounted and continued his northern trek.

As man and horse ascended out of the valley, they were about a half-mile from the ridge when gunfire erupted. "Must have run into some Comanches," Dan said to his horse. He pulled the Winchester .44 from the saddle boot and put the gelding into a trot.

Cresting the ridge, Dan saw a blue cloud of hanging smoke as guns thundered in crashing crescendo across the desert. He sat stunned, momentarily studying the drama being enacted on the bank of the river below.

There was not an Indian in sight. Troopers were killing troopers in a bloody, heated battle. The waters of the Rio Grande were stained a faint crimson color, shimmering in the sunlight.

For a moment, the blond man on the black horse sat in perplexity. It was his nature to join in a fight. He was ready to do so, now. Men in the river were squared off against men on the bank. But who were the good ones and who were the bad ones? Rushing into the conflict headlong might get him shot by both sides.

Dan studied the situation. Men were falling like poisoned flies. The troopers on the bank seemed fewer in number. Within minutes, it was evident that two men were fortified in the rocks and four or five were now encircling them.

Inborn in the soul of Dan Colt was the inclination to help the underdog. Right or wrong, it was four—no—*five* against two. Dan would side with the two. Raking the horse's sides, he thundered down the slope.

As he came within a hundred yards, he skidded to a stop and slid from the saddle in one smooth motion. Levering a shell into the chamber, he shouldered the rifle and sighted in on the nearest rider encircling the rocks. Dan squeezed the trigger. The man toppled from the horse's back and lay in a motionless heap, his head twisted grotesquely under his body.

Suddenly the other four were aware of what had

happened. Dan fired again. The slug caromed off a boulder, screaming angrily.

Joe Caraway threw a quick glance at the man shooting from the slope. He was too far away to make out his features, but the rifle belching fire was enough. "Let's get out of here!" he shouted to the others.

In a moment, the four rounded the river bend, galloped over a rise, and vanished.

Swinging into the saddle, Dan rode to the cluster of boulders where Lieutenant Puter was assisting the bleeding colonel to the ground. Allen was cursing Joe Caraway vehemently.

Easing the wounded man to a sitting position against the base of a boulder, Puter turned to face Dan Colt as the tall man dismounted. "Mighty glad you showed up, stranger," said the lieutenant, extending his hand. "I'm Lieutenant Puter. Richard Puter."

"Dan Colt."

Releasing Dan's hand, Puter gestured toward Allen. "This is Colonel—Did you say *Dan Colt?*"

The colonel looked up, eyes widened. Puter's face registered the shock in his brain.

"Yep," replied Colt.

"*The* Dan Colt?" Puter said in amazement. "The gunfighter?"

" 'Fraid so," said Dan.

"I remember your name from Texas, Oklahoma, and Kansas. Never thought I'd ever get to meet you!"

Kneeling down, Dan said, "You hurt bad, colonel?"

"Bullet went clear through," grimaced Allen. "Main thing is to get the bleeding stopped."

Turning to Puter, Dan said, "Mind if I work on

him, lieutenant? I've had some experience with this sort of thing."

"Go right ahead, Mister Colt," said Puter. "I'll check and see if any of these men out here are alive."

CHAPTER FIVE

By noon Dan Colt had cleaned and bandaged Colonel Jeffrey Allen's shoulder. The left arm was in a makeshift sling. Allen cursed the pain in his shoulder, but even more he cursed the names of the deserters who had escaped. Joe Caraway, Ken Deere, Alex Hopper, and Frank Stevens had made a clean getaway.

Sitting up, his back braced against a boulder, the colonel looked at Dan Colt with hard eyes. "You sure the shoulder is broken?"

"No, sir," replied Colt, "but it looks like it is. The doctor at the fort will have to diagnose it."

"Somebody's got to go after those yellow-bellied deserters," hissed Allen, shifting his position to ease the pain.

"It's a cinch you can't do it," said Dan dryly.

"Main thing, now, is to get you to Doc Springston at the fort," put in Lieutenant Puter.

The colonel swore again. "Caraway and his bunch

are riding away with eight thousand dollars of government money."

Puter, who hunkered near the colonel, stood up and said, "Not quite, sir." Wheeling, he walked to his horse and raised the flap on one of the saddlebags. Allen watched him warily as he returned holding a packet of ten-dollar bills.

Allen blinked. "What the—?"

"It's all in the saddlebags, colonel," said the muscular lieutenant, smiling.

The colonel ran a hand over his heavy gray moustache. "But Tim Baker had the money. I saw him go down. There was too much smoke to see clearly, but somebody took Baker's horse."

Puter's face lost some of its color. What he was about to admit to his senior officer could go hard on him. "Well, you see sir . . . Baker and I switched saddlebags when we bedded down last night."

"What for?" snapped Allen, his eyes flashing.

"Well . . . I . . . uh . . . just had a feeling that something was awry, colonel. So I told Baker to switch with me."

Allen's face went crimson. "You mean you knew this mutiny was going to happen and you didn't tell me?"

"I didn't *know* it was going to happen, sir," retorted Richard Puter, "I just had a gut feeling about Caraway."

"Why didn't you tell me about it?" bellowed Allen.

"I had nothing to offer as proof, sir. You will agree that for me to accuse Sergeant Caraway without something concrete would be a mighty serious thing."

Allen readjusted the sling, gritting his teeth. "Well,

I guess you're right about that," admitted the colonel. "But if you felt strong enough about it to switch saddlebags, I should have been advised."

"Yes, sir," said the lieutenant, nonplussed.

"Seems to me," interjected Dan Colt, "you oughtta be glad he switched the bags, colonel. What could you have done about the situation if Puter had told you?"

Glaring hotly at Colt's intrusion, Allen said bitingly, "I'd have confronted Caraway, that's what!"

"You don't think he would've admitted it, do you?" retorted Dan.

The colonel gave the tall, blond man a blank stare.

"At least, you've still got the money," said Colt. Turning, he let his gaze drift over the dead men lying on the ground and along the bank of the river. One horse lay dead among them. "What about these bodies, colonel?"

"We'll take them all back to the fort," replied Allen. "The horses must be somewhere near."

Dan set his eyes on the surrounding desert, squinting against the molten sun. "They're scattered somewhat, but we can gather them up."

"Lon Ward's horse dragged him across the river, colonel," said Puter advisedly, "then took off running. I doubt if we ever find horse or man."

"We won't have time to search, anyway," put in Colt. "We've got to get this man to the fort."

Within an hour, the scattered horses with the letters "U.S." branded on their rumps had been gathered. Each animal had a corpse draped over its back, lashed to the saddle. One horse carried two corpses.

Colonel Allen was hoisted into his saddle by Puter

and Colt. As the lieutenant mounted his own horse, he said, "Funny thing about Lon Ward."

"What's that?" asked Allen, adjusting his weight in the saddle.

"He had to have been in on the revolt. Yet, at the last minute, he shouted the warning."

"Conscience was probably burning his guts," said the colonel idly.

"Does it have to go in the report about his being with Caraway's bunch, sir?"

"We'll just write it up like it happened," Allen answered flatly. "We'll let the big brass draw their own conclusions."

"I was thinking about his parents, sir..."

"You have to take the good with the bad in this life, Puter," Allen said, firming his jaw.

"But, sir, he saved your life."

Allen's face turned to granite. His eyes flashed red. "Ward was a *deserter*, lieutenant. The only thing lower than a deserter is a dead snake's belly."

"We'd better get moving," interjected Dan Colt. "There's sixty miles between us and the fort."

Under the clear, burning sky the caravan of corpses plus three living men moved slowly northward. The sun slammed invisible bolts of fire on their backs.

Hours passed. Twice they stopped to water the horses in the Rio Grande. The colonel grew more irritable with every mile. His shoulder was beginning to bleed again. The pain was becoming unbearable.

In the dead heat of midafternoon, both Richard Puter and Dan Colt were busy scanning the land for signs of Indians when Colonel Allen suddenly peeled off his horse head-first. The horse nickered as the big man struck the ground. Puter bounded from the saddle, scrambling to Allen's crumpled form.

Dan Colt dismounted stiffly. As he approached, Puter looked up and said, "He must've fainted. Now the wound is bleeding bad."

There was a stand of willows on the river bank about fifty yards ahead. Pointing toward them, Dan said, "Let's get him down to the trees."

Stretching the unconscious colonel on the grass in the dappled shade of the trees, Dan worked on the crude cloth compress. Allen was beginning to come around as the adept hands of Dan Colt checked the bleeding. Blinking his glazed eyes, the colonel said, "What ... happened?"

"You passed out, colonel," said the tall man. "Hit the ground pretty hard. Shoulder was spewing blood. I got it stopped again, but you're not traveling any further today."

"Now listen, Colt," snapped Allen, "I can make it. We've got to—"

"You'll bleed to death if that wound comes open again," cut in Dan. "Best thing for us to do is let you rest till morning. Puter and I will find a way to make a travois. You'll travel the rest of the way lying down."

Allen knew Dan was right, but his fuming hatred for Joe Caraway was eating at his patience. The quicker they got to the fort, the sooner something could be done to begin the search for the deserters.

Looking up at Dan from his prone position, he said, "Make the travois right now. Let's keep moving."

"Colonel, you're white as a sheet. You've lost too

much blood. If we wait till morning, you'll be in better shape to travel."

Allen swore.

"Go ahead and cuss to your heart's content, colonel, but that's the way it's going to be," said Dan firmly. With that, he wheeled. Motioning to Puter, he said, "Let's ground rein the horses and relieve them of their load."

The red ball of fire was settling over the western horizon when Colt and Puter, who sat with backs to trees, noticed that Colonel Jeffrey Allen was waking up. He had napped for three hours.

At first, the big man rolled to his side, moving groggily. Suddenly, a stab of pain cleared his head. Looking around and focusing on the lieutenant, he said, "Puter, come help me. I want to sit up and lean against a tree."

Puter jumped at the colonel's words and soon had him braced against a willow, taking water from a canteen. Allen scowled at Dan Colt. Dan flashed him a retaliating smile.

"Don't smile at me," snapped Allen. "We could be a lot closer to the fort if it weren't for your pigheadedness."

"Yeah," breathed Dan, removing his hat and laying it on the grass. "With another dead man flopped over a saddle."

Allen went mute, set his jaw, and stared into the sunset. His thoughts were instantly on Joe Caraway and the other three deserters who were somewhere north, riding free. Hatred boiled like molten lava inside him. He would see them shot. All four of them. He would personally command the firing squad. But first, they had to be tracked down, caught, and returned to Fort Ryan.

In the dim light of dusk, Colonel Allen studied Dan Colt. Looking at his handsome features, he said, "Colt, I've been trying to remember all the things I've heard about you."

Dan looked at Richard Puter, adjusted his position against the tree, and threw his gaze at the big gray-haired man. "Don't believe more than half of it, colonel," he said dryly, "bad or good."

"Fast with your hands."

Dan eyed him in the waning light, but said nothing.

"In a fistfight or a gunfight," added Allen. Cocking his head, he asked, "How many men you killed?"

"Lost count," answered Colt.

"You were a bounty hunter, weren't you?"

"For a while," Dan said, a touch of irritation in his voice. "It was a living."

"Came up against some tough *hombres*, I bet."

"A few."

"Who was the fastest man you ever killed?"

"Slick named Vic Baron."

"*Baron?*" echoed Allen.

"*Baron?*" re-echoed Puter. "You drew against Vic Baron?"

"Yep."

"Why, I heard tell there was nobody faster'n Baron," said Allen with amazement.

"There's always somebody faster," said Dan flatly.

Darkness descended over New Mexico, bringing with it a cool breeze and a canopy of twinkling lights overhead. The three men ate army rations and some beef jerky provided from Dan Colt's saddlebags. A fire was too risky. Instead of coffee, they drank water.

A coyote yelped somewhere in the distance.

A plan was formulating in Colonel Jeffrey Allen's brain. Turning his eyes toward Dan Colt, though he could barely make out his form in the dark, he said, "Colt, in your bounty hunting . . . you ever set out to track down an outlaw you didn't get?"

"Only once," responded Dan.

"*Once?*"

"Yep. Fella knew I was on his trail. Didn't want to face my guns *or* prison. Killed himself. Jumped over a cliff up in Colorado. Never did find his body. Went down in a dark crevice. Did all that tracking for nothing. Can't collect a bounty without a body."

"Listen, Colt," said Allen, breathing heavily. "The government puts up a reward for the capture of deserters. I don't know how much it'll be, but if you'll go after Caraway and his bunch, I'll see that it's worth your while. You bring them in for the firing squad, I'll put a thousand dollars of my own money on top of the reward. Even if you bring them in dead, I'll do it. Just rather have them alive to sweat out a firing squad."

"Sorry, colonel," said Dan. "I'm on a tracking mission of my own."

"Oh?"

"My brother."

"You're trailing your brother?"

"Yep. My identical twin. He's an outlaw."

"You mean you're after your twin brother . . . to turn him over to the law?"

"Yes, but there's more to it than that."

Allen clucked his tongue. "I'd like to hear about it."

"Yeah, me too," chimed in Richard Puter.

Dan paused. "It's a long story, gentlemen."

"Let's hear it," said Puter.

"According to your own words, we're not going anywhere till morning," the colonel reminded Dan.

"Okay," said Colt.

Jeffrey Allen was not particularly interested in the story, except to find some loophole where he could persuade Dan Colt to give up the pursuit of his brother long enough to track down and bring in Joe Caraway and his three cohorts.

Dan leaned back against the tree where he sat and stared at the starlit sky. "When I was about three years old," he began, "my parents were traveling in eastern Arizona. I don't even know if they were headed east or west. A gang of outlaws attacked them. I was apparently off playing somewhere. I have a vague recollection of peering at the scene through some bushes. The gang murdered my parents, took all our valuables, and rode away."

Puter and Allen listened in silence as Dan proceeded. "A man and woman came along traveling from California to Texas. Ben and Katie Mason. They buried my parents and took me with them to Texas. Raised me."

"What about your twin?" asked Allen.

"I'm coming to that," replied Dan.

"What made you become a gunfighter?" asked Puter.

"Coupla fellas gunned down Ben Mason," Dan said, a touch of ice in his voice. "I was just a kid, but

I got a little instruction from the right man and strapped on a pair of guns. I tracked 'em down and challenged 'em."

"Put 'em both away, huh?" queried the lieutenant.

"Mmm-hmm. Found out I had a natural knack for the guns. One thing led to another. Challengers seemed to come out of the woodwork. The more men I killed, the more I had wanting to prove they could outdraw me. I hired out as bodyguard a few times. Then took up bounty hunting. Traveled the West. Took on challengers as they came. Then, in Wichita, I met Mary."

"She changed things, I bet," said Puter.

"Considerably. We got married, moved to Wyoming. Bought a ranch in the Rockies, west of Laramie."

"Hung up your guns," said Allen. It was a statement. Not a question.

"Yep. For five years."

"Five years?" echoed Richard Puter. "After ranching that long, why did you—?"

"I'm about to tell it," butted in Colt. Bitter memories raced through Dan's head. Tight-lipped, he continued. "One day I had driven my wagon to Laramie for supplies. Only went to town 'bout every three—four months. Met up with three scummy drifters on the road. Passed the time of day with 'em and drove on home."

Dan's jaw clenched hard. His voice tempered cold. Cold as an arctic wind. "When I got home, I found Mary shot to death. My hired man had also been shot, but was clinging to life by a thread. He lived long enough to describe those three filthy drifters."

"You strapped on your guns and went after them," said Richard Puter.

"Yep."

"Caught 'em where?" asked Colonel Allen.

"Trailed 'em to Holbrook, over in Arizona. Met two of 'em on the street. Killed 'em both."

"What about the other one?" asked the lieutenant.

"Don't know where he was that day, but I'll tell you about him a little later." Dan took a swig from his canteen. "After I shot it out with those two killers, the town marshal put a gun on me. Arrested me as one *Dave Sundeen*, who had been in Holbrook a few weeks before. There'd been a gunfight in one of the saloons. Dave Sundeen had killed two men. When the marshal, whose name is Logan Tanner, tried to arrest him, he shot the marshal."

"Dave Sundeen is your twin," said Allen.

"Uh-huh. Only I didn't know it then."

"You didn't know you had a twin brother?" queried Puter.

"You'll understand better in a moment," Dan said to the lieutenant's vague form in the darkness. "I stood trial as Sundeen and was sentenced to five years at Yuma."

Allen swore. "Couldn't you prove where you were at the time Sundeen shot Tanner?"

"Nope. Mary and my hired man were the only two who could have done so. And they were dead."

Allen swore again.

"While I was in Yuma prison, they mated me with an old convict who turned out to be one of the gang who had robbed and killed my parents. It was he who told me that on the day they did it, they took a little blond-headed boy named *Davey* with them. He ended up with a family named Sundeen."

"You mean you didn't remember him?" asked Puter.

"I vaguely remembered a little towheaded playmate, but that's all. Like I said, I was about three. I might have only been two."

Richard Puter shook his head in the dark.

"So," continued Dan, "I broke out of Yuma and started trackin' Dave. Logan Tanner is now a U.S. marshal. He's hot on my trail this minute. He has never accepted the twin story. He thinks I'm Sundeen. Has a personal goal to put me back in Yuma."

"So you are after Dave to turn him over to Tanner," said Allen.

"Yep. I hate the situation, but the law will breathe down my neck until I can clear myself. Only way I can do it is to produce my twin."

"You have not seen him, then, since you were little?" asked Puter.

"Nope."

"Do you think he knows about you?" It was the colonel, this time.

"Existing, or trailing?"

"Either."

"Nope."

"I take it he's headed north along the Rio Grande," said Allen.

"Right," said Colt.

"What about the third killer?" asked Puter.

"Oh," said Dan, "I caught him over near Silver City."

"Gun him down?"

"Nope."

"You didn't kill him?"

"I killed him."

"What with?"

"My fists."

"Oh."

All was quiet for several moments. Colonel Jeffrey Allen spoke up. "You wouldn't leave Sundeen's trail long enough to earn yourself a big reward?"

"Trail would get cold," replied Colt. "Besides, Tanner's breathin' down my neck. If he catches me before I find Dave, I'm a cold turkey. I *have* to stay after Dave."

The three men agreed it was time to get some sleep. The lack of movement had eased the pain in the colonel's shoulder. Sleep came easily. Just before he dropped off, Allen said under his breath, *I'll find a way, Mister Colt. I need your talent and experience to bring in Caraway. Don't you worry. I'll find a way.*

CHAPTER SIX

Sergeant Joe Caraway had not heard Dan Colt's rifle fire, but when Lester Worth toppled from the horse, his gaze swung out on the dusty slope. There stood a man next to a large black horse, blue smoke sifting from the muzzle of his rifle.

The eyes of the other three deserters quickly followed Caraway's finger as he pointed toward the interfering rifleman. The stranger fired again. The slug caromed off a boulder, screaming angrily. Caraway looked toward the spot where Puter and Allen were crouched. They were well protected among the rocks.

Caraway threw a quick glance at the man shooting from the slope. He was too far away to make out his features. Reining his horse around, he shouted to the other dissidents. "Let's get out of here!"

Gouging their horses' sides, the four deserters rounded the river bend and galloped over a rise. As they rode side by side, Ken Deere hollered, "Joe, we shouldn't leave Allen and Puter alive!"

Turning toward Deere, his hat brim flattened against the crown, Caraway bellowed back above the thundering hooves, "Just keep ridin'! Allen's hurt bad. They'll be a long time gettin' him to the fort. We'll be in Santa Fe by then!"

The four men in blue put five miles between themselves and the bloody scene at the river bend before stopping to blow their horses. Dismounting on the river bank, they pulled heavily from their canteens and refilled them.

"What now, Joe?" asked Alex Hopper.

"We'll cross the river right here, move west a couple miles, and head for Socorro. Captain Radmacher may get nervous and send out a patrol lookin' for Allen. We sure don't want to run into that patrol."

Deere, Hopper, and Stevens snickered, eyeing each other furtively.

Caraway swore. "Why did that stranger have to come along and kill Worth? We would look more like a real detachment with five men. Most everybody knows the army never sends out less than five men together."

"We'll just have to make the best of it," put in Frank Stevens.

Caraway sighed heavily. "We'll take both banks in Socorro tomorrow morning. We should make it there before noon. Then we'll ride north, cutting the telegraph wires in several places. It'll take 'em a week to find the breaks and fix 'em. By that time we'll have cleaned out the banks in Santa Fe, cut some more wires, and be in Colorado."

"We oughtta run into a coupla Wells Fargo stages and a coupla Burlington stages by then, too," said Ken Deere.

"Main thing we gotta do is not run into any Comanches," said Caraway. "Those red devils could mess up this whole operation."

Allowing their horses a brief drink, the four deserters mounted and rode across the river. As they climbed the bank on the opposite side, Frank Stevens, astride Tim Baker's horse, said, "There's one good thing about Lester's gettin' shot, Joe."

"What's that?" asked Caraway, casting a backward glance.

Stevens patted the saddlebags tenderly. "We only have to split this eight thousand dollars four ways."

A wide grin spread across Caraway's tanned face. "That's what I like about you, Frank. You always see the bright side of everything."

The four men had a good laugh and rode northwest, the blasting sun on their sweaty backs.

The afternoon wore on. Having reached a point some two miles west of the rolling Rio Grande, the four riders aimed straight north. Talk was minimal.

As the sun began its downward slant in the west, Alex Hopper lifted a finger and pointed northeast. "Look there, fellas," he said sharply. "Indians."

About a mile east of the river was a band of Comanches, riding south.

Joe Caraway pulled his mount to a halt. The others followed suit. Squinting to focus, Caraway said, "Looks like about six or seven of 'em. They're leading some . . . Oh. They've got some dead ones.

Must've run into one of the patrols. I think there's a dozen or more horses."

"Yeah," said Stevens. "Looks like about half of 'em's packin' corpses."

"Do you think they see us?" asked Hopper.

"Don't think so," said Caraway. "Even if they did, I doubt they'd bother us. Looks like they're bent on gettin' home."

The men in blue traveled until the sun had disappeared behind the western rim of the earth. They made camp on a tributary creek that fed the Rio Grande, where there were willow thickets and cottonwoods.

"We made good time this afternoon," said Joe Caraway, loosening the cinch on his saddle. Lowering the saddle earthward, he spoke with optimism. "We'll make Socorro easy by noon tomorrow. Then we can add to what's in Baker's gear."

At the same moment, Frank Stevens swung Baker's saddle from the horse's back and plopped it on the ground. "Let's just have a look-see at our big fat payroll," he said with glee. Dropping to his knees, he unbuckled the flap on one of the saddlebags, as the others gathered around, smiling.

Stevens felt a cold wave wash over him as his fingers closed around underwear, socks, shaving gear, and cartridges. The bag contained food rations and coffee. Stevens twisted on his haunches and looked up into Joe Caraway's face. The smile was gone.

"Where's the money, Frank?" said Caraway stiffly.

Stevens swallowed hard. "Why . . . I . . . uh . . ."

"You grabbed the wrong horse, Frank!" bellowed Ken Deere, eyes bulging.

Stevens stood up, shaking his head. "No . . . no. I shot Baker. When he fell off, I got on. This is Baker's horse!"

Alex Hopper started to say something, when Joe Caraway took one step and chopped Stevens in the mouth. The man half stumbled over the saddle and went down. In seething anger, the tall sergeant leaped through the air, pouncing on Stevens. The latter, having gained his senses, fought back. The two men rolled down the bank of the creek, Caraway cursing furiously.

As they came to their feet, Frank Stevens sent a hissing fist into Caraway's mouth. Stevens was shorter than the sergeant, but outweighed him ten pounds. Caraway staggered. Stevens hit him again. The blow was solid, like the sound of an ax hitting an oak tree. Caraway went down, his mouth moistened with blood. He rolled to his feet next to the slapping water of the creek and wiped his hand across his lips. He eyed the blood on his hand and glared at the other man with heated passion.

The sergeant let out a wild yell and charged. Stevens set himself and swung a haymaker. Caraway was bent low and the punch bounced off the top of his head. Caraway's shoulder plowed into Steven's midsection. Air whooshed from his lungs as the two hit the ground. Rolling, punching, cursing, they splashed into the creek.

Hopper looked at Deere. Deere raised his shoulders, pursed his lips, and shook his head. "Leave 'em be, Alex. Just let 'em fight it out."

Both fighters were now on their feet in the knee-deep water, fists thrashing violently. Caraway caught Stevens flat-footed with a solid belt to the jaw. The shorter man fell beneath the surface of the water. As he came up coughing and spitting, the taller man jumped on his back, shoving his head into the water. Stevens fought back, but could not get his face clear to breathe.

Standing on the bank, Alex Hopper shouted, "Joe! Let him up! You'll drown him!"

The blond Caraway held his opponent in the water and flashed Hopper a wicked smile.

Suddenly, Caraway felt himself being lifted upward. Stevens had him on his shoulders. Coughing, the shorter man slammed Caraway hard on the creek bank.

The sergeant was momentarily stunned. Stevens kicked him in the mouth, saying between sputters and coughs, "You tried to drown me! You dirty—"

Without finishing his accusation, Frank kicked Caraway in the groin, as the man rolled on the bank. Staggering to him as he howled, Stevens sank his fingers into the sergeant's shirt and dragged him into the creek. Getting a fistful of blond hair, the shorter man bobbed Caraway's head into the water and held it there.

The sergeant fought and splashed to no avail. Frank's grip was firm. Caraway's efforts were dwindling.

Ken Deere, standing on the bank with a worried look, shouted, "That's enough, Frank! Don't kill him!"

Stevens smiled. "I won't. I just want him to think I am!"

With that, Stevens lifted the sergeant out of the water and laid him on the bank. It was Caraway's turn to cough and sputter. Frank sat down beside him. It took a full ten minutes for Joe Caraway to gain control of his breathing and sit up.

The two men eyed each other in the gathering darkness. "Look at it this way, Joe," said Frank. "If this fight had started earlier in the day, we would have worked up quite a sweat. At least fightin' in the creek, it's cooler."

Joe touched his battered lip with his fingertips and chuckled.

"Besides that, even though they switched saddlebags on us, we've got extra underwear," said Stevens with a half-smile.

Caraway chuckled again. "That's what I like about you, Frank," he said. "You always see the bright side of everything!"

Caraway broke into a hearty laugh. Stevens joined him. The other two suddenly caught the humor of the moment and together the foursome had a good, long laugh.

At high noon the next day, citizens of Socorro, New Mexico, looked on with admiration as the four cavalry troopers rode down the street. Their backs were straight, faces fixed forward, sabers shining in the sun. Casually, the men in blue reined in at the hitchrail in front of the Socorro County Bank.

Alex Hopper unsnapped the flap on his holster and halted at the door as the others entered the stuffy, overheated bank. While Hopper's eyes scanned the sun-drenched street outside, Joe Caraway tossed a glance at two customers standing at the teller's window. Moving past them, he walked to the little fenced area where two dignified men sat at desks.

The younger one, who was closest to the gate, eyed the chevrons on Joe Caraway's sleeve. Smiling, he said, "Good afternoon, sergeant."

"Good afternoon," said Caraway pleasantly.

Frank Stevens stood just inside the door. He would bar the customers from leaving.

Ken Deere paused about halfway in the room, eyes taking in the whole scene.

"Is one of you gentlemen the president?" asked the tall, splendid-looking sergeant.

The older man scraped his chair on the wooden floor and stood up. "Yes, sergeant," he said, stepping around the desk, "may I help you? I'm Morton Potts, president of the bank."

Outside, a man dressed in a business suit came along the boardwalk. Alex Hopper tried to appear relaxed and casual. Stepping past him, the man gave him an estimable look and passed through the door. Once inside, his eyes fell on the other uniformed men. Frank Stevens moved close to him and whispered, "Please stand still and be quiet, sir. There's gonna be a robbery here in a minute." The man blinked and looked around.

"Yes, Mister Potts," Caraway was saying, "to keep someone from robbing the bank, we're going to take the money for safekeeping."

Potts slowly moved his head back and forth. "I don't understand, sergeant, I—"

Caraway's revolver was instantly out, the muzzle lined on Morton Potts. The latter's jaw slacked.

"I said we're going to take the money for safekeeping in case somebody decides to rob the bank today."

The two customers at the teller's window, a man and a woman, turned to leave. The woman gasped as Ken Deere thumbed back the hammer of his revolver. The couple froze in their tracks. Looking past them to the teller, who was still unaware of the situation, he said, "You there in the cage. Grab a big sack and empty your cash drawer into it."

The teller's eyes widened and showed a hint of rebellion until he threw a glance at Caraway holding a gun on Potts. Instantly, he obeyed.

"Now, gentlemen, let's go into the vault and put all of the cash in a nice big sack, okay?"

While Caraway herded the frightened bank executives into the vault, ex-Trooper Deere relieved the stunned couple of their cash and jewelry. Frank Stevens was accepting the latest customer's wallet, when he shouted, "Hey, Joe, what's takin' you so long?"

The sergeant's voice came from the vault, "Just about got it!"

Twenty seconds later, Caraway emerged from the vault, carrying a heavily loaded sack. "Let's bring 'em all back here," he said, tossing his head toward the vault.

The teller glared hotly at Deere as he handed him the sack. "I'll see that your commanding officer hears about this."

"Now, you just do that, bucko," sneered Deere.

Morton Potts was trembling. "If you lock us in the vault, we'll all suffocate," he said nervously.

"I didn't know I looked that dumb," retaliated Caraway.

"Huh?"

"I know what those little holes up by the vault ceiling are for, sir," snapped Caraway.

Potts's face flushed.

"Now, I want you to write down the combination to the lock for me, okay? I'll put it in the top drawer of your desk. You'll be out of there by sundown, I betcha."

With shaky hands, the president of the Socorro County Bank scribbled the words, *vault combination*, followed by left and right numbers. Crowding customers and bank personnel into the vault, Joe Caraway slammed the door and spun the dial. Folding the piece of paper, he jammed it into his shirt pocket.

"Wait a minute, Joe," said Frank Stevens. "You told the man you would put it in his desk drawer."

A cynical look froze on Caraway's face. "Changed my mind," he said caustically, walking past Stevens.

Frank sank his fingers in Caraway's arm, spinning him around. Anger flared in his eyes. "Put the paper in the drawer, Joe." Stevens breathed it, rather than voicing it.

Caraway waggled his head, moving toward the desk. "Just thought I'd keep the combination for future use."

"They'll change it anyway, Joe," said Deere, trying to ease the tension.

" 'Spose so," said Caraway. "Let's get outta h—"

Abruptly, the door opened. Two men walked in. Caraway could see Alex Hopper's face behind them. He looked flustered and worried.

One of the men was tall and well dressed. The

other was short, stocky, and clad in a blood-speckled butcher's frock. Being engrossed in conversation, it took them a moment to realize things were not right.

"The bank's closed, gentlemen," spoke up Joe Caraway, holding the sack of money in one hand and his gun in the other.

"But you can leave your money with us," added Ken Deere. "After all, if you can't trust the United States Cavalry, who can you trust?"

Scowling heavily, the two men gave up their money.

The tall one looked at Caraway. "When they lock you up, I hope they lose the key."

The sergeant's revolver came across the man's face with a savage blow. He crumpled to the floor.

Setting his gaze on the butcher, Caraway said, "And you? What do you hope?"

The stocky man's eyes widened. "N-nothing, sir. I—"

Caraway raised the gun as if to strike him. "Don't call me *sir*, mister. I'm only a low-paid sergeant."

The man recoiled and blinked, expecting to be hit.

Alex Hopper stuck his head through the door. "Hey! Will you dudes hurry up! What are you doin' in there?"

"Keep your shirt on," snapped Caraway, "we're comin'." Turning back to Deere and Stevens, he said, "Let's tie 'em up and get over to the other bank."

In less than three minutes, the four men in cavalry blue were riding casually up the street in the early afternoon sun. Swinging to the hitchrail of the First Bank of New Mexico, they dismounted.

CHAPTER SEVEN

While Dan Colt built a smokeless fire and started the coffee, Colonel Jeffrey Allen leaned against a willow tree and watched the sunrise.

Richard Puter crudely tied saddle blankets together and, breaking limbs off the trees, made a travois. By the time the sun had detached itself from earth's rim and began to float skyward, the caravan of corpses was under way.

Riding his own mount, Lieutenant Richard Puter led the colonel's horse, to which the travois was attached. Allen lay on the tautly stretched blankets, his face set in grim lines. Clutching his wounded shoulder, he grimaced when the travois ran over rocks and hard places. Still, he admitted to himself, this was easier than sitting in a saddle.

The faces of Joe Caraway, Ken Deere, Frank Stevens, and Alex Hopper hung in his mind like chunks of foul, spoiled meat. He would not rest until those four excuses for human beings died in a hail of bullets at a firing squad.

The big colonel's red-rimmed eyes roved among the corpses that dangled over the horse's backs. He felt bad for the good men who were cut down by Caraway's murderous followers. A warm feeling of satisfaction swept through him as he eyed the five deserters whose dead hands hung downward, swaying with the movements of the four-legged beasts that carried them.

He thought about Lon Ward. The lieutenant was right. Ward *had* saved his life. No doubt Caraway's first shot was intended for him. Ward took it by calling out. Allen wondered if Ward's horse was still wandering the sun-baked desert, dragging the battered corpse of its rider.

Dan Colt and Lieutenant Richard Puter rode in relative silence, speaking only on occasion. Each twisted in his saddle periodically, to check on the wounded cavalry officer.

Dan looked at the blue-shadowed Sandia Mountains carved against the crystal sky in the distance. He wondered if Dave was still headed north. Maybe there would be some kind of clue in Socorro.

His eyes roamed the land around him. Almost unconsciously he looked for signs of Comanches as he admired the singular beauty of this part of the desert. Lacking the red earth and rock formations so familiar in Arizona, still there was a rugged charm in this raw country. Broken by jagged, wandering canyons and narrow washes, it was decorated by black chaparral and desert flowers of purple and yellow. Highlighting it all was the winding ribbon of water known as the Rio Grande, with carpets of green lining both banks.

Several stops were made to water the horses and give the colonel a chance for relief from movement. Dan could see that the travel was taking its toll on the man.

About an hour before sundown, Dan Colt was just about to rub his weary eyes when something caught his attention in the red distance. Horses were silhouetted against a low range of hills.

"Hold it," said Dan, pulling on the reins. The caravan came to an abrupt halt.

Colonel Jeffrey Allen rolled his eyes, tilting his head back.

Weakly, he said, "What is it, Colt?"

"What do you see?" enjoined Puter.

"Horses," Dan said, standing in the stirrups, studying the northern horizon.

"I have binoculars in my saddlebags," offered Allen.

"I'll get them," said Puter, slipping to the ground. Returning quickly, he lifted them to Colt, who still stood in his stirrups.

"Thanks," said Dan, lifting the binoculars to his eyes. Turning the tiny wheel in the center, he adjusted the focus.

Allen and Puter waited patiently for Dan's comment. Then it came. "Comanches." He waited for a few seconds. "Headed this way."

"How many?" queried the colonel.

"There's seven sitting up . . . and . . . three . . . four . . . five . . . *six* draped over horses."

"Must've been some cavalry up there somewhere," said Puter.

"Could have been a patrol looking for us," Allen said from his nearly prone position.

"One thing for sure," observed Dan. "They're heading straight for us. We sure don't need a Comanche fight right now."

Colonel Allen was gripping his shoulder. "Will we ... meet them before dark, Colt?"

"No, sir," replied Dan. "By 'right now,' I meant on this trip. If they stop at sundown and we do too, we'll be about three-four miles apart. We'll sure meet 'em head-on about seven o'clock in the morning."

"Let's cross the river and keep going in the dark," said Allen.

"Too risky, colonel," said Dan. "You've about traveled all you can for one day."

The colonel's voice was weak. "We sure can't stand off seven walleyed Comanches, Colt."

Dan was still peering through the glasses. "I don't think we'll need to, colonel. They've stopped. They saw us."

Allen swore.

Lowering the glasses, Dan studied the scene ahead with his naked eyes. "I've got an idea, colonel."

"What's that?"

"They don't have glasses. All they can tell from there is that we are a column with a string of horses. It's too far for them to tell that these horses are carrying dead men. When I look at them without the glasses, all I can distinguish is a string of horses."

The colonel swore again. "If they've spotted us, we're dead men if we don't get away in the dark."

"You're a dead man if we try that," said Dan sharply.

"What's your idea?" asked Puter.

Pivoting in the saddle, Dan swung his gaze to the rear. "That last place we watered . . . with the cottonwood trees..."

"Yeah?"

"It's only a half-mile back. Let's turn around and go back there."

The colonel cursed again, shaking the travois. "What do you want to backtrack for?"

"I'll explain when we get there," said Colt. "C'mon, lieutenant, let's turn this parade around."

Darkness had fallen by the time Dan Colt and his strange caravan had gained the thicket of cottonwood trees on the bank of the river.

"You make the colonel as comfortable as possible," Dan said to Richard Puter, "then jump in and help me gather firewood. We'll need to light five or six fires and keep them burning till about ten o'clock. In the meantime, we've got to use the pack hatchets from the troopers' gear and cut fourteen limbs."

Overhearing the directions Dan was giving the lieutenant, Colonel Allen spoke weakly. "What are you going to do, Colt?"

Stepping near the travois, Puter on his heels, Dan said, "Colonel, we have fourteen dead men riding thirteen horses, correct?"

"Yes."

"You are riding the travois, so your saddle is empty, correct?"

"Yes, yes, I can count. What's your plan?"

"First thing we'll do is light a wide circle of fires.

Make us look like a confident platoon camping for the night."

"All right," said Allen. "Go on."

"Puter and I will cut limbs from the trees. Before sunup, we'll run the limbs down the back of each man's uniform and under his belt. With the same ropes that now hold them to the saddles, we'll tie their hands to the pommels. The limbs will hold them erect, so it'll look like they're living men sitting in the saddles. If you were seven Comanches taking your dead home for burial, would you light into a platoon of sixteen troopers?"

The colonel took a deep breath. He would have laughed, except for the pain it would cause. "Colt, if you bring this off, I'll see that they make you a general!"

Lieutenant Puter laughed and said, "I'll vote for that! Let's get you situated, colonel, so I can help Dan get those fires built."

While the two young men built fires and chopped limbs, Colonel Jeffrey Allen promised himself that one way or another, Dan Colt would soon be on the trail of Joe Caraway and company.

At the gray hint of dawn, Colt and Puter finished bracing the fourteen corpses in the saddles.

Testing the balance on each one, Dan said, "We'll have to move real slow, lieutenant. It wouldn't take much of a jolt to swing them out of the saddles."

"All we have to do is convince these Comanches and we can lay them across the horses again and head for the fort," said Puter.

At sunrise, breakfast under their belts, the three living men and their "platoon" headed north. Dan Colt rode in the lead carrying the binoculars. The sun had been up about an hour when he fixed his gaze straight ahead, then lifted the glasses to his eyes.

"See 'em?" asked Richard Puter.

"Yep."

"They coming this way?" asked Colonel Allen from the travois behind.

"Yep."

"Have they spotted us yet?" asked the colonel.

"Nope. But they will."

Fifteen minutes passed. The bizarre caravan topped the ridge of a gradual rise, giving the Comanches a grotesque skyline view of the "fighting men." Through the glasses, Dan saw the Indians stop and stare.

"See anything?" asked Allen.

"Yes, colonel."

"What?" asked Puter, narrowing his eyes, trying to make out the reaction of the Comanches.

"They're pulling off the trail!" said Dan, a lilt in his voice. "They're heading east."

Puter subdued a yell, closed his fist, and swung it hard through the air. "You did it, Colt! Your idea saved our skins!"

"They're moving fast, colonel," said the tall, blond man.

"Congratulations, *General Colt*!" said Allen excitedly.

As soon as Dan was certain the danger was past, he stopped the caravan and once again positioned the corpses belly-down over the saddles. The colonel's

BANDITS IN BLUE

wound was looking worse. Dan knew that haste was of the essence.

The relentless sun burned down upon them, forcing frequent stops for water. Though it cost them precious time, Dan was glad for the Rio Grande. He had fought the sun on occasion across Arizona—where there was no river.

It was midafternoon when Lieutenant Puter spotted them. "Look, Dan," he said, pointing due north.

Lifting his eyes, Colt saw them. Black, circling sentinels of death. Whirling shapes of doom, high in the azure sky.

"Vultures mean only one thing," said Puter.

"Yeah," agreed Dan. "I'm afraid it'll be that patrol who killed the six Comanches . . ." Sleeving sweat from his brow, he continued, " . . . and was wiped out by the seven."

Within the half-hour that it took to reach the spot, the vultures were on the ground, digging their hooked beaks into human flesh. At the appearance of the sixteen horses, they screeched, spread their wings, and eased themselves skyward.

There were nine troopers sprawled in a sand-strewn arroyo. The Comanches had stripped them naked and savagely mutilated their bodies.

Lieutenant Puter examined the clothing. "They're from A Company out of Ryan," he said to Colt, who still sat on his horse. "But they've been mutilated so bad I don't know if I can identify any of them."

"Any way to tell by the uniforms?" asked Colonel Allen from the travois.

"Only that they were A Company and what their

ranks were," replied Puter, sifting through the clothing. "Leader was a lieutenant. Could be one of three men. There was a sergeant and a corporal. The rest were privates."

Slipping from the saddle, Dan Colt said, "I see some of their horses scattered around, lieutenant. Do you want to round 'em up and take the bod—what's left back to the fort?"

Richard Puter's stomach was churning. As he turned, Dan saw the whiteness of his face. "I'm not sure, Dan." Walking wobbly-legged to the colonel, he said, "What do you think, sir?"

"It would be cruel for any of the wives or children to see this mutilation, Puter. I know it's hot and you men are tired, but immediate burial is the only answer."

By sundown, the bodies lay in a common grave. The lieutenant quoted scripture and voiced a few choice words over the mound.

"Let's camp by the river," said Puter. "I don't like this place."

That night the three men sat on the river bank under the stars, leaning against a large rock. The stars winked overhead.

"We'll be at the fort by sometime tomorrow afternoon," said the lieutenant. "I'm sure dreading the report I have to give Captain Radmacher. All these men dead. Some of them *deserters*."

"I don't know Radmacher, lieutenant," said Allen. "What kind of man is he?"

"The best, sir. A fine officer. You'll like him."

Turning his attention to Dan, Allen said, "Thought any more about it, Colt?"

"What's that, colonel?" asked Dan.

"My offer."

"You mean about going after the deserters?"

"Precisely."

"Not really. I've got to pick up Dave's trail and get back on it."

"I'll still put a thousand dollars with the normal reward."

"Doesn't the government have some kind of special group of men to go after them?" asked Dan.

"No," replied the colonel. "They will hire a Pinkerton man to do it."

"*One* man?"

"That's right. It's his job to find them, then invoke aid from local law authorities to effect the arrest."

"Works pretty good that way, huh?"

"Most of the time," said Allen. "Would be a lot better in this case if you'd go after them."

"Sorry, colonel, but I've got to get Dan Colt cleared with the law before I take any jobs."

CHAPTER EIGHT

As the four U.S. cavalry deserters approached the door of the First Bank of New Mexico, Alex Hopper said, "Don't you birds take so long this time. Somebody will spot the trouble at the other bank before long. We gotta light a shuck outta this town."

"You just guard your post, Hopper," sliced Joe Caraway.

The sergeant was first through the door, followed by Deere and Stevens. There were no customers in the bank. As the teller looked up through the brass bars and smiled, Ken Deere approached the window. "What can I do for you, trooper?" asked the elderly gentleman.

Joe Caraway heard the teller gasp, as he headed for the executive area. Neither of the two desks was occupied. As he stepped through the wooden gate, a middle-aged man emerged from the vault carrying a cardboard box. The man saw the blue uniform and smiled. Then his line of sight fell on the black muzzle. The smile drained away.

"Let's get all the money out of the vault, mister," snapped Caraway.

Outside, Alex Hopper saw a tall, stately man angling across the street. He was coming from the hotel restaurant, working a toothpick in his mouth. From a side street, a lean young man on a chestnut mare approached him and stopped. The two men chatted in the middle of the street. Hopper saw a glint of sunlight come from the badge on the mounted man's shirt.

The ex-trooper felt cold prickles dance on his spine as the marshal dismounted and walked his horse to the hitchrail, sided by the tall man. While the two stood talking, the lawman eyed the four horses with the army brands. He shot a glance at Hopper, smiled, and nodded. Hopper nodded back, his heart skipping a beat.

Suddenly, the three robbers plunged out the door, guns drawn, money sacks in their hands.

The tall, stately man said something Hopper could not distinguish. The marshal made a half-turn, going for his gun. Caraway spotted him, raised his gun, and fired. The lawman's weapon discharged, the bullet plowing dust. As he went down, the older man bent over and retrieved the revolver. Caraway shot him through the head before he could bring the gun to bear.

As the four men in cavalry blue swung into their saddles, people were beginning to swarm the street like ants that have had their hills disturbed.

Morgan Hill

"Let's head south!" said Caraway. "We'll turn north later."

As they galloped down the dusty street, a man in a buckboard lifted his rifle. Ken Deere and Alex Hopper both shot him at the same time.

Riding hard, the foursome soon were out of sight. They veered off the road into a deep arroyo and stopped. As the dust settled, Joe Caraway glowered at Alex Hopper with fire in his eyes. "Why didn't you warn us about that lawman?" he snapped.

"There was no way I could," retorted Hopper defensively. "He was lookin' straight at me!"

"Forget it, fellas," interjected Ken Deere. "Alex had no control over the marshal showin' up."

Swinging his horse around, Caraway said, "Let's ride the river for a while. Then we'll pull out and head north. It'll take 'em awhile to form a posse."

Gouging their horses' sides, they rode out of the arroyo, crossed the road, and headed for the river. They rode south down the middle of the Rio Grande for over an hour, then ascended the west bank in a rocky area. Riding west till the river was out of sight, they took a straight course north.

By midafternoon, the four dissidents passed the parallel line with Socorro and angled back to the river. They watered the horses and rested in a shady spot on the bank.

"Want to count the money now, Joe?" asked Hopper.

"Naw, let's put some more miles behind us and count it when we camp for the night," replied Caraway. "We need to get back to the road and cut the telegraph lines. Sooner or later that posse will figure out we didn't go south."

"Oughtta be a coupla stages we can stop between here and Albuquerque," put in Frank Stevens.

Ken Deere laughed. "Boy, are we gonna be rich!"

The stageline road ran parallel with the Rio Grande at an average distance of half a mile—from Santa Fe, south through Albuquerque, to Socorro. It followed the river from Socorro to Fort Ryan, then left its green banks and took a straight line for Las Cruces. At that point, the stagecoaches turned around and headed north again. Communications were kept up to date by the telegraph line which ran along the entire route.

While his friends sat their horses and watched, Ken Deere shinnied up the telegraph pole with a pack hatchet under his belt. Looking around from his vantage point, he saw no movement on the desert. Wielding the hatchet, he chopped the wire. It whined as it was severed.

An hour later, Deere was aloft, cutting his sixth wire, when he saw a cloud of dust on the road due north. The dust took on a red hue from the setting sun.

Squinting for better focus, he saw a weaving stagecoach with a six-up span of horses lunging into the harness.

"What're you lookin' at?" asked Joe Caraway from the ground.

"Stagecoach," replied Deere. "In a real hurry."

"Prob'ly tryin' to make Socorro before dark," mused Frank Stevens audibly.

"Yeah," enjoined Alex Hopper, "there's bandits on this road. Could be real dangerous at night."

Everybody laughed.

"Come on down, Ken," said Caraway. "Let's stop the stage and relieve them of that burdensome money they might be carryin'." As they mounted, he said, "Now, fellas, don't pull your guns till I do. Leave your flaps loose and be ready. Let me do the talkin'."

The men in army blue rode slowly up the middle of the dusty road, four abreast. The stage rounded a bend and the driver immediately saw them. Yanking back on the reins, he pulled the vehicle to a stop in a cloud of dust.

Passengers leaned from the window to see why the driver had stopped. A woman's voice came from within. The four men picked up the word "troopers." Caraway wondered where the shotgunner was.

"Sergeant, are we glad to see you!" bellowed the driver. "We wuz robbed back the road apiece. A lone bandit. Shot my gunner. He's down in the coach, bleedin' bad!"

Caraway tossed his men a look of caution and dismounted, saying, "Let me take a look at him, driver."

The driver, a leather-faced man in his midfifties, scrambled down and opened the coach door. Two women and a well-dressed man stepped out. One of the women was young and pretty. The other was older and quite obese. She wore a large plumed hat. Immediately, the fat woman barraged Joe Caraway with insistent demands that he pursue the bandit and retrieve her money and expensive brooch.

"Calm down, Mrs. Fortney," said the driver. "The sergeant wants to look at Herb."

The wounded shotgunner was leaning slackly in the right rear corner of the coach. His shirt and vest were stained with blood from a bullet hole in his upper arm. He was breathing heavily.

Caraway crawled inside and examined the arm without touching it. A strip of petticoat was wound tightly around it. "Did the bullet go clear through?" Joe asked.

The shotgunner, a man about the driver's age, nodded. "Yeah. Clear through."

Turning to the driver, who was leaning in the coach, the sergeant said, "Looks like the bleeding is checked for the moment."

"Thanks to Miss Wells, here," said the driver, arching a thumb over his shoulder at the pretty young lady who stood between the fat woman and the prosperous-looking man.

Caraway set his eyes on the fair-haired girl and smiled. "You did a good job on the arm, ma'am."

Marla Wells managed a weak smile. "Thank you, sergeant."

Backing from the coach and straightening to full height, Caraway spoke to the driver. "He'll be all right till you get him to Socorro. How much did the bandit get?"

"Cash box with thirty-five hundred dollars, plus the pocket money of meself and the passengers. He also took Miss Wells's diamond engagement ring and old lady—er ... Mrs. Fortney's brooch."

This was the big woman's cue to start in again. Which she did.

"Now, wait a minute," said Joe Caraway. "We're not lawmen, Mrs. Fortney, but we're heading north and if we see this man, we'll apprehend him. If not, we'll alert the authorities in Albuquerque. Now, let's have a description."

Everybody started at once. "Hold it. Hold it," interrupted Caraway. "Driver, you tell me what he looked like. If there's anything these others want to add, they can do so when you're finished." Turning toward the three men in blue who still sat their horses, he said, "You men listen close. We want to know exactly what this man looks like."

All three knew what their leader had in mind.

"Tall and blond, sergeant," began the leather-faced driver, "like you . . . only taller and blonder. Looked to be 'bout six-five or so. Wore a heavy moustache. Had a flat-crowned brown hat with one o' them neck cords. Big fella. He'd weigh well over two hundred. Packed a pair o' twin Colts, tied down at the thighs. You know . . . like a gunhawk."

"And extremely handsome," put in Marla Wells. "Like a stage actor."

"Meaner'n a snake, too," came the shotgunner's voice from inside the coach.

"He would not have shot you," said the well-dressed man, "if you had done as he told you."

The shotgunner cursed.

"What kind of horse was he ridin'?" Caraway asked the driver.

"Big buckskin gelding."

Joe Caraway's glance touched each face. "Anything else?"

No one answered.

"Okay," said the sergeant. "We'll be on the lookout

and if nothing else, we'll give the description to the law at Albuquerque. You do the same at Socorro."

"Oh, we'll let Miss Wells do that, sergeant," said the driver with a wide smile. "She's engaged to Ben Travers, the marshal at Socorro."

Joe Caraway felt a line of white heat stab through his system, searing his insides with guilt. His eyes met the girl's fleetingly, then rested on the driver's face. "Better hurry and get your man into town."

The men in blue watched the stage disappear in a cloud of dust.

Alex Hopper shook his head. "Too bad what that pretty young thing is gonna face when she gets to Socorro," he said in a sad tone.

"You think you killed that marshal, Joe?" asked Ken Deere.

"Yeah. Think so," said Caraway. "Hit him dead center in the chest."

"Too bad. Nice girl," put in Frank Stevens.

Joe Caraway swore. "She oughtta know better than to get herself involved with a lawman. Women like that oughtta marry men who don't live by the gun. It's her own fault."

No one was sure if the sergeant meant what he said.

"Let's move out," said Caraway sharply, heading for his horse.

"We got a problem, Joe," said Ken Deere, swinging into the saddle. "Everybody in Socorro will know we're headin' north, once that stage gets there."

"True," admitted the sergeant, "but they'll have to wait till the posse gets back to tell 'em. We've got a good enough head start. We'll pop the lines a few more times, too. Keep the telegraph crippled. Right now, we gotta concentrate on findin' the tall, handsome bandit with the cash box."

It was sundown twenty-four hours later, when Ken Deere spotted the lone rider from atop the telegraph pole. The man was about a half-mile ahead, watering his buckskin in the Rio Grande.

"Hey, Joe," called Deere.

Joe Caraway was drinking from his canteen. Lowering it and smacking his lips, he said, "What is it?"

"Our man is up ahead, watering his big buckskin horse in the river."

Caraway smiled and pulled on the canteen again. "Good. We'll get him by morning."

The men in blue agreed that the tall, blond bandit had been traveling wide of the beaten path, but of necessity had to take his mount to the river for water.

"Stay up there and watch which way he goes," commanded Caraway. "We'll find where he camps and take him at first light."

Ken Deere hugged the pole and watched the tall man mount and ride north, then angle east toward the Sandias. He lost him as the last glimmer of daylight succumbed to the night. When Deere's feet touched the ground, he looked at the three dark shadows that hovered near. "He's gonna camp in the mountains. We better get goin'."

As the four rode abreast, the evening sky blossomed into sharp focus, shimmering milky white. It wasn't long until a big yellow moon appeared behind the rugged Sandias and presently drifted skyward. By the time the men in blue reached the foothills, it was a silver disc, lighting the desert a soft blue-white.

Climbing higher, the foursome glimpsed the Rio Grande far below in the moonlight, winding southward like a silver cord.

"You're sure this was the path you saw him approach?" Joe Caraway asked Ken Deere.

"Absolutely," replied Deere. "He'll be up here somewhere."

Reaching a high sharp crest among some tall evergreens, the four dismounted and walked to the edge. Reading the rugged country below in the moonlight, each man studied it for signs of a campfire.

"I don't see a thing," said Alex Hopper.

"Me neither," said Frank Stevens.

"He'll light a fire when he thinks he's safe," put in Joe Caraway. "Probably nothin' in these mountains but coyotes, cougars, wolves, the tall bandit, and us."

At that moment an owl hooted from a nearby tree.

"And *owls*," added Stevens.

"We'd get a broader view from that lower spot down there," suggested Ken Deere, pointing. "This rock formation to the left blocks some of the lower areas."

Agreeing that Deere was right, they led the horses down a steep path for some two hundred feet. The path leveled out at the designated spot. Tying the horses to some slender birch trees, the four men moved out on a flat rock some thirty feet from the path.

Patiently, they waited, scanning the moon-flecked mountains below. Time seemed to drag.

Then, Ken Deere slapped Caraway's arm and

pointed. Far below, among a cluster of giant pine and spruce trees, a tiny orange light flickered.

"That's him!" exclaimed Hopper, the youngest of the four. "And there's our thirty-five hun—"

"Not so loud, you idiot!" scolded Caraway hoarsely. "Sound carries in this thin air somethin' fierce. You want him to—"

Joe Caraway's words were cut short by the nicker of one of the horses. Instantly, all four were nickering and prancing nervously. Their pounding hooves were slinging rocks over the sheer precipice at the edge of the path, the rocks cascading noisily to the rugged depths below.

"Get ahold of 'em!" said Caraway just above a whisper. "Somethin's spooked 'em!"

Each man reached his horse, gripping the bridle with all his strength. The frightened animals, eyes wide in the moonlight, fought to be freed.

Suddenly, the source of their fright appeared on a rock ledge some thirty feet above them, to the west. Silhouetted against the milky sky was a large cougar, ejecting a hiss that evolved into a shrill roar. The sheen of its coat, even the whiskers, took on the silver of the moon. The slender tail moved slowly back and forth.

Ken Deere, fighting his horse with one hand, slipped his carbine from its boot with the other.

"No! Wait a minute, Ken," said Caraway. "If you fire that gun, we'll lose that thirty-five hundred dollars!"

"If I don't," argued Deere, "we'll lose our horses ... maybe our own lives!"

The cat stood stiff-legged. It had not crouched to pounce. Again came the angry hiss, the shrill roar.

"He would jump the horses if it weren't for us," said Frank Stevens, wrestling his mount. "Cats have a natural fear of man. I think if we could hit him with some rocks, he might run away."

"Worth a try," agreed Caraway, "but how do we let go of these frightened beasts long enough to heave rocks at the cat?"

"The trees are flexible," said Stevens. "Wrap the reins tight and close. If we all do it at once, two can hold the horses while two throw rocks."

The big cat stood his place, hissing and roaring while the four men pulled the horses' muzzles close to the slender trees, wrapping the reins tightly. Hopper and Deere held the horses while Caraway and Stevens picked up sharp, fist-sized rocks and hurled them with all their strength at the cougar.

The wild beast howled fiercely when struck with the first rock. Dodging back from the edge, it appeared again, pawing at the air. One of the rocks slammed its tender nose savagely. The cat let out a shrill cry, reared, and clawed the air again. Then, abruptly, it wheeled and disappeared.

The horses immediately began to settle down.

"He's gone," said Stevens.

"Wheeeew!" breathed Hopper. "There for a minute I thought we all might be cat meat!"

Though the mountain air was cool, the men in blue wiped sweat. Returning to their perch, they saw the fire still winking far below.

"Hope he didn't hear anything," said Deere.

"If he did, it was all animal noises," remarked Joe

Caraway confidently. "He knows the cats are around. That's why he's got a fire."

The nefarious four peered through the trees at the gray of dawn. The buckskin was turned rump-forward, rubbing its neck on a tree. Next to the barely smouldering fire was the blanketed form of the stagecoach bandit. Head on saddle, hat tipped low over his face, he lay in silence.

Leaving their horses so as not to allow the buckskin to catch the familiar scent, they tiptoed over the pine needles, guns drawn.

"If his horse nickers," whispered Caraway, "draw a bead on the man and hold it. If he goes for his gun, kill him."

The morning breeze touched their faces, telling them they were downwind from the buckskin. The big horse would not smell them.

Easing up to the inert form on the ground, smoke from the dying fire whirling around his legs, Joe Caraway lined the muzzle on the tilted hat and eased back the hammer. The other three formed a semicircle around the sleeping figure.

Caraway bellowed, "All right, cowboy—stand up!"

The form did not move. Caraway was preparing to drive a boot into the man's ribs when a cold voice from behind the semicircle spoke. "I *am* standing up, big mouth!"

The foursome whirled.

Dave Sundeen stood indomitable on a large boulder, tall against the morning sky. His twin Colts were leveled on the bandits in blue. The muzzles resembled two dark, menacing eyes. The morning breeze ruffled the blond locks on his hatless head.

"Now you apes can gamble . . . or drop your guns. I guarantee I'll take out two of you. The other two might get lucky. On the other hand, maybe not. One way to find out, if you've got the hankerin'."

CHAPTER NINE

Fort Ryan came into view late in the afternoon. As they crested a gradual rise, the first thing to meet Dan Colt's gaze was the red, white, and blue flag waving in the hot breeze.

Slowly, the entire compound became visible. Squat adobe buildings, bleak and drab, were surrounded by a tall stockade wall. As they drew closer, Dan could see tumbleweeds piled against the west wall of the fort. The desert wind had a way of rolling them across the surface of the river and driving them the hundred-yard span to rest at the base of the vertical poles.

Sentries standing on the ramp behind the wall were waving their arms. One by one, more heads appeared, some studying the approaching caravan through binoculars.

The big gates of heavy timber swung wide to receive them. As they moved inside, Dan's eyes fell on deep ruts in the sun-baked parade ground, cut by the wheels of the water wagon on its endless trips to the Rio Grande.

Lining both sides of the parade were the adobe buildings. They were old and the adobe was peeling off the walls, exposing the vertical logs underneath.

Captain Peter Radmacher emerged from his office and stood momentarily stunned as he eyed the long line of horseflesh bearing fourteen dead troopers. Quickly, his line of sight fell to the travois and the pallid face of Colonel Jeffrey Allen.

The afternoon wind gusted through the fort, popping the flag atop the pole and sending swirls of dust across the parade.

Radmacher's glance swung to Lieutenant Richard Puter and the tall stranger who rode the big black. Stepping from the porch, the captain approached the caravan as it halted in front of the infirmary.

Someone hollered for the physician. Dr. George Springston's worn and leathered face appeared in a dirty, fly-specked window. Seconds later, he came through the infirmary door carrying a worn and cracked leather bag.

Swinging from the saddle as troopers began to gather, Lieutenant Puter said, "Back here, Doc. It's Colonel Allen."

Springston and Radmacher arrived at the travois at the same moment. Whispered words of shock and bewilderment filled the air. Pained exhaustion branded Allen's face, tracing deep lines around his eyes and mouth. The lowering sun was full in his face. His eyelids were squeezed half-shut against the flaring shaft of light.

Morgan Hill

Doc Springston took one look at the colonel and spoke to the crowd. "Some of you men pick him up and carry him into the infirmary. Go easy. He's in a lot of pain."

As Allen was carried into the building, the captain turned and spoke to Richard Puter. "Comanches, lieutenant?"

"No, sir," replied Puter.

"Then, what . . . who—?"

"Deserters."

Radmacher swore vehemently.

"They were led by Sergeant Caraway, sir. Some of the dead ones here were with him. I'll give you a full report right away. There are three other deserters with Caraway. Troopers Deere, Stevens, Hopper. They'd have killed the colonel and myself if it weren't for this man." Puter gestured toward the tall, blond man with the twin Colts thonged low on his hips.

"Captain Radmacher . . . Dan Colt." As the two men clasped hands, the lieutenant said, "Dan came on the scene as we were shooting it out. He killed Lester Worth and the others hightailed it."

Looking Dan in the eye, Radmacher said, "Much obliged for your intrusion, Colt." The captain squinted, cocking his head to one side. "How did you know who to shoot?"

Dan grinned. "Didn't. Just picked the underdogs and started shooting at the upperdogs."

Looking back at Puter, Radmacher said, "We sent a patrol out for you. They must have missed you."

Lieutenant Puter lifted his hat and ran a bandanna over his bald pate. "They never got that far, captain. Comanches wiped 'em out."

Radmacher's jaw slacked. "Oh, no."

"The devils mutilated 'em so bad, sir, we went ahead and buried the remains."

Radmacher swore. "They've hit us twice here since you've been gone. They're cutting us down, thinning our ranks. I expect them to come like a swarm of hornets any time."

Captain Peter Radmacher was a man in his early forties. He stood six feet tall and weighed in at just under two hundred pounds. He was every inch a soldier. Though a veteran of many Indian campaigns, worry was etched on his rugged face. Turning toward the infirmary, he said, "Let's check on the colonel."

Dan Colt followed the two officers into the infirmary. Immediately he was met with the strong odor of antiseptics and various medicines.

Colonel Allen was lying on the examining table, his teeth clenched in pain. An open salver of disinfectant sat on a small table next to a pan of hot, bloody water. Springston was working on Allen's shoulder with nickel-plated probes.

"Don't come too close, men," said the doctor, not looking at their faces. As he continued examining the wound, he spoke without looking up. "Colonel tells me you cared for his wound, Mister Colt."

"Yes, sir," said Dan.

"You ever had medical training?"

"Nope."

"Well, you did a good job, son, for what you had to work with. You should have been a doctor."

"Is the shoulder broken, doctor?" asked Dan.

"'Fraid so. Collarbone's broken . . . shoulder dislocated."

"I thought it was."

"I'm going to have to put it in place before I suture the wound," said Springston, turning toward the three men. "I need you to hold him down while I—" He stopped short, his eyes lined on Dan's face. "Your name *Colt* or *Sundeen*?"

Dan's heart leaped to his throat. Little prickly needles raced up and down his spine.

Before Dan could find his voice, the physician said, "How's your back?"

"Let's get this done and I'll talk to you about it," said Dan.

Within thirty minutes the colonel's shoulder was in place and the wound stitched. Allen was under the influence of a strong sedative and almost out.

Richard Puter, satisfied with the colonel's condition, said, "Captain, I'm a little bushed. If it's okay with you, I would like to go bathe and stretch out for a while."

"Certainly, Puter. You can give me an oral report in the morning. Then we'll put it in writing."

Puter saluted, then looked at Colt. "See you later, Dan. Thanks for helpin' us underdogs and stickin' with us all the way."

The tall, muscular man smiled. "My pleasure, lieutenant."

Richard Puter closed the door behind him. "Fine officer," said Radmacher.

Dan nodded. "Sure is."

Doc Springston was scrubbing blood from his hands at a washstand. Looking over his shoulder, he said, "Now, Mister Dan Colt, why did you tell me less than a week ago that your name was Dave Sundeen?"

BANDITS IN BLUE

Relief was washing over Dan, just to know that he had not lost Dave's trail. "It *was* Dave Sundeen you saw a few days ago, doctor," said Dan advisedly. "I'm his twin."

Doubt registered on the physician's face. "I've seen a lot of identical twins in my time, son," he said, looking over the tops of his half-moon glasses, "but there's always some distinction. Now, who you trying to bamboozle?"

The captain looked on in bewilderment as Dan said, "Doctor Springston, if I prove to you that I'm not the man you saw a few days ago, would you sign an affidavit before the captain, here, that twins exist?"

"You've got me confused a little, son," said Springston, drying his hands, "but if it'll help you, I'll sign it . . . providing you've got proof."

Removing his hat and hanging it on a coat tree, the tall man slipped out of his vest and commenced to unbutton his shirt. "What did Dave Sundeen come by here to see you about?"

"Gunshot wound in his upper back. Was having some discomfort with it. Wanted me to look at it."

"Did you?"

"Of course."

Shirt off, Dan wheeled, exposing his back. "See it?"

Fort Ryan's eminent physician breathed an oath. Shaking his hoary head, he said, "Proof enough. I'll sign anything you want. But I sure don't understand all this."

"I'll explain it later, sir," said Dan. Looking at Radmacher, he asked, "When the doctor signs the affidavit, captain, will you attest it with your signature?"

"Of course, Colt, but I'm confused, too. I didn't see your twin when he came to the fort. It was night. He was in and gone quite rapidly. Sentries at the gate saw him, but other than that, only doc, here. But . . ."

"Mmm-hmm?" hummed Dan.

"Why is your name Colt and his name Sundeen?"

Eyeing the doctor, then swinging his gaze back to the captain, Dan said, "Can the three of us eat supper together?"

Radmacher nodded. "Certainly."

"I'll explain it all then."

After a hot meal of steak, potatoes, beans, bread, and army-style coffee, Dan poured himself a fresh cup and began his story. The three men were alone in Radmacher's quarters. The aging physician leaned on his elbows and listened. The captain bit the tip off a cigar and flamed it into life. Rocking his chair on the two back legs, he billowed smoke and fastened his eyes on the handsome blond-headed man.

The evening wore on.

"So . . ." said Dan in conclusion, "when U.S. Marshal Logan Tanner trails me here, I want you to tell him about Dave's wound. That will convince him that twins *do* exist and that he sent the wrong man to Yuma Prison. With the signed affidavit, he and I can ride to Holbrook and clear my name."

"So you're planning to stay here till Tanner shows up?" asked the captain.

"Absolutely, sir, if that'd be okay. He can't be more than a week behind me. Maybe less."

"After what you did for our men, you're welcome

here as long as you want to stay," said Radmacher, studying the red tip of his cigar. "You might have to do some Indian fighting. The attacks are coming every few days."

"Don't mind that at all, captain. I've fought a few in my time."

"Hope your U.S. marshal makes it through those bloodthirsty Comanches," said Springston.

"Me, too," said Dan with a tight smile. "Funny. I haven't felt this way about Tanner before. But now that I can jam solid proof of Dave's existence down his throat, I can't wait for him to show up."

Outside on the parade, the bugler sounded the signal for lights out. Dan was ushered to a cot in officers' quarters and was asleep instantly.

Reveille sounded at five thirty. Breakfast was over by six thirty. As Dan walked to the stable to check on his horse, he noted that the ramp was lined with men on all four sides. Clearly they were expecting an attack.

The attack did not come.

In early afternoon Dan went to the infirmary to check on Colonel Allen. Doc Springston was cleaning an arm wound sustained by a trooper in the last Comanche attack. A small, gray-haired woman was feeding broth to the colonel, who was braced up on a cot.

Allen's eyes lined on Colt's tanned features. "Ah, there you are," he said, after swallowing. "I was about to send for you."

The woman looked at the tall man, smiling. Dan removed his hat.

"Colt, meet Mrs. Fanny Herndon," said Allen. "She helps doc by coming in and adding a woman's touch to this crude infirmary. I sure was glad to see her."

Springston tossed the colonel a hard look.

"Howdy, ma'am," said Dan, grinning widely. "My name's Dan Colt."

"It's a pleasure to meet you," replied Mrs. Herndon. "Our new commanding officer, here, has been telling me about you."

"Don't listen to it, ma'am," said Dan. "He has a way of stretching the facts."

"You been thinking about my offer?" asked Allen.

"Nope."

"You're the man for the job, Colt. With your experience and expertise with those guns, you could bring the filthy skunks in."

"Colonel, the doctor over here has given me what I need to bring my nightmare to an end. My twin was here in the fort less than a week ago. He was shot in the back a couple months ago in Tombstone. The wound was givin' him some trouble. He stopped to have doc take a look at it. Don't you see what this means?"

Dan ran his fingers through the thick hair on his head. "I told you about Logan Tanner trailin' me. He'll be along in a few days. He wouldn't pass the fort without stopping in. Doc can testify to Tanner about Dave's wound. I don't have one. Now I can clear up this mess!"

A slow, sinking feeling settled over Allen. The burning hatred for the deserters boiled inside him. If the right man was not soon on their trail, they might never be caught.

"I'll draw up that affidavit for you yet this afternoon, Dan," offered Springston.

"Thanks, doc."

Allen scowled. "What affidavit?"

"Doc's gonna put his testimony about Dave and me on paper," said Dan, "so Tanner can present it to the authorities in Arizona and clear me with the law. Captain Radmacher is going to attest doc's signature." The elation inside Dan Colt was clearly visible in his sky-blue eyes.

Colonel Jeffrey Allen's brain was spinning. "I'll tell you what, Colt," he said, readjusting his position on the cot, "you light out after Caraway and his bunch . . . and I'll personally put the affidavit in Tanner's hands. Guarantee it. I'll also wire the general at El Paso and get you the highest reward possible. Could be a thousand dollars a head. And I'll raise my personal ante to two thousand. Dead or alive."

"Colonel," said Colt, "it's worth a million dollars to me just to see the look on Tanner's face when he finds out I've been telling the truth. I'm stayin' right here till he comes."

Allen cursed, his face flushing with frustration. "But those stinking snakes will get away if somebody doesn't get after them right now!"

"Wire for a Pinkerton man," snapped Dan. "This is my chance to be cleared. I'm not gonna muff it. I'm gonna be right here when Logan Tanner rides in."

Allen's face grew redder. He raised up on one elbow.

Doc Springston crossed the room to the colonel. "You better settle down, colonel," he said firmly, "or this fort will be writing for another new commanding officer." Turning to Colt, he said, "You'd better go, Dan. He needs to rest. I'll see that you get the paper by this evening."

"Sure, doc," responded the tall man. "See you later." Stepping to the door, he turned. "Nice to have met you, Mrs. Herndon."

"Likewise, I'm sure," said the woman.

Throwing his glance to the cot, he nodded, donned his hat, and said, "Colonel."

As the door clicked shut, Allen said, "Doctor, I want to see Captain Radmacher immediately."

"I'll get him for you immediately," said Springston.

"Good," breathed the colonel, easing back on the cot.

"Immediately after you take a long nap," Doc said flatly. "You will take your sedative now."

Allen's eyes widened and turned pink around the edges. "I am the commanding officer of this fort, Doctor Springston. You get me Captain Radmacher this instant. That's an order!"

"Give him his sedative, Mrs. Herndon," said the physician, returning to the wounded trooper.

"I'll have you court-martialed, Springston," hissed the irate colonel.

"You need to consult the United States Army Code Book, sir," retaliated Springston calmly. "Article forty-seven, section D-nine. It clearly states that when an officer is seriously wounded or ill to the degree that the attending physician deems him incompetent, the attending physician may overrule or disregard any orders given by that officer. You'll find it on page three-hundred-three, two-thirds of the way down the page."

Allen's mouth gaped.

"Now," said the doctor, "I so deem. You shut up, take your medicine like a good boy, and go to sleep."

"But—" gasped the startled colonel.

"Outside of an all-out Indian attack, there can't be any emergency that pressing. I'm trying to keep you alive, colonel. Now, do as I told you."

That evening, Dan ate in the officers' mess hall with Lieutenant Richard Puter. The latter was happy to learn of the sudden turn of events concerning Dave Sundeen.

As Captain Peter Radmacher finished his meal taken in his own quarters, there was a rap at the door. "Come in," called the captain without getting up.

The door creaked on its hinges as Doctor George Springston's lean body came into view. "Captain, the colonel has just woken up from his nap. He wants to see you right away."

"Thanks, doc, I'll come right over."

As the physician turned to leave, he spied the affidavit lying on the captain's rolltop desk.

Nodding his head and rising from the table, Radmacher said, "I'll take it to Colt after I see what Colonel Allen wants. Let's walk over together."

Crossing the parade, Radmacher eyed the sentries on the wall ramps, silhouetted against the night sky. Upon entering the infirmary, Doc Springston raised the wick on a low-burning lantern and filled the room with light.

Morgan Hill

Seeing the captain, Allen's countenance cleared.

"You wanted to see me, sir?" asked Radmacher.

"Yeah, about four hours ago," snapped Allen, scowling at Springston.

"The doctor is merely looking out for your well-being, sir," said Radmacher in Springston's defense.

"I would like to speak with the captain in private, doctor," the colonel said crustily.

"You're the commanding officer, sir," replied Springston with a fleeting smile. As he passed through the door, he said, "Ring if you need me."

Setting a desperate gaze on Radmacher's face, Allen said, "Have you signed that affidavit for Colt yet?"

"Yes, sir."

Allen ejected several foul words.

"But I haven't given it to him yet," said the captain. "Why?"

"I don't know quite how yet," answered the colonel, relief in his voice, "but I'm going to find a way to use that affidavit as a lever to send Colt after those deserters."

"But, sir—"

"He's the man for the task, Radmacher. He's got to do it." Allen's eyes were wild.

"Yes, sir," said the captain.

"I haven't seen my office yet. Does it have a safe?"

"Yes, sir."

"You have the combination, I assume?"

"Yes, sir."

"Lock that paper in my safe, captain."

"But, sir, Doc can still tell that U.S. marshal about Sundeen."

"I need a little more time, yet," said Allen. "I'll figure something out. You just lock that paper in my safe. Keep this between you and me. That's an order."

CHAPTER TEN

Dan Colt was awakened at dawn by the sharp blast of a bugle. It was not reveille. It was the battle signal.

As he dressed hastily, Dan could hear doors slamming in the barracks, men shouting, and Captain Radmacher barking orders. The officers who had slept in this same room were already outside. Strapping on the Colts and thonging them to his lean, muscular thighs, he grabbed his rifle, slapped on his hat, and bounded out the door.

The morning sky looked like pink buttermilk. As Dan stepped on the parade, Radmacher spied him. "Colt! East ramp!" cried the captain.

Dashing across the open ground to join the men who were scrambling up the east ramp ladder, Dan suddenly heard the savage war whoop of the Comanches. Gaining the ramp, he found a slot between two troopers and crouched low. The yelping Comanches were riding hard, closing in from three sides. Dan assumed they were coming from the west, also.

At one corner of each ramp stood a lieutenant, ready to give the order to fire. Richard Puter was in command of the east ramp. He stood with a saber in one hand and his service revolver in the other.

The Indians were within a quarter of a mile now. Dan worked the lever on his Winchester .44. The painted ponies raised a cloud of amber dust, carrying the screeching savages across the flats. As they pulled within a hundred yards, they cut loose with their rifles.

At fifty yards, Puter yelled, "Fire!"

Colt already had a bead on a yelping Comanche. The rifle bucked in his hands. The red man stiffened with the impact of the bullet, then rolled off the horse.

An arrow hissed, struck a pole near Dan's head, and vibrated for a few seconds. Guns were belching flame, filling the air with acrid blue smoke.

Dan could hear Radmacher yelling at the women of the fort to pull their heads out of the windows and close the shutters.

On the ground below, the smoke cleared with the shifting breeze, exposing a painted Comanche about to release an arrow. Dan lined the rifle muzzle on the red man's chest and squeezed the trigger. He was a split-second too late. The bowstring thrummed. In less than a heartbeat the arrow of the dead Indian pierced through the throat of the trooper to Dan's left. The man dropped his rifle and stood erect, clutching at the arrow. He made an awful gagging, choking sound. Blood bubbled from his mouth. He staggered forward and peeled over the wall, hitting the earth with a muffled thump.

Several of the screaming Comanches left their horses and were trying to scale the wall. Others were circling on horseback, firing feather-decorated rifles. There were white lateral streaks of clay beneath their eyes. Their naked chests and bellies were striped with red and yellow paint. They wore breechcloths of buckskin and beaded doeskin moccasins.

The ones on foot were slashing head-on for the walls, trying to find footholds in the rough timber.

As Dan squeezed off more shots, he noticed a warrior making his way up the wall directly beneath him. The savage had a knife between his teeth, ready to use when he topped the wall. The tall man waited until the Indian's head appeared at the top and his fingers curled over the edge. Slamming one hand brutally with the rifle butt, Dan yanked the knife from his mouth. While the Comanche tried desperately to cling to the wall, Dan drove the blade into his neck. Spewing blood, the Indian slid down the wall.

The battle waged on. Troopers were being killed and wounded in the noisy, smoke-filled fracas. As Dan dropped his head beneath the top of the wall and knelt on the ramp to reload his rifle, he spotted Doc Springston on the rutted parade tending to the wounded.

As Dan returned to resume firing, he heard the deadly swish of an arrow as it sped past his right ear. He had killed two more of the yelping Comanches when the trooper to his right howled and collapsed on the ramp. The man had a bullet in his shoulder. Grimacing, he rolled from side to side.

Directly below the ramp there were two troopers picking up a wounded man. "Hey, soldiers!" Dan yelled. As they paused and looked up at him, he said, "There's another one up here. When you come back, I'll lower him to you."

Both troopers nodded and carried the man to Doc Springston. Lowering him tenderly to the ground, they ran back to the ramp. "All right," said one, "ease him down to us."

Dropping his Winchester, Dan gripped the wounded man under the arms and lowered him feet-first. As he released him into waiting hands, he caught sight of Captain Radmacher standing on the west ramp. Apparently the lieutenant in that position had fallen and Radmacher had taken his place. At the same instant, the captain buckled, staggered backward, and toppled from the ramp. Dan noted that the west wall had been thinned considerably.

Dropping his rifle barrel back in the crotch between two poles, Dan continued shooting. Several moments passed. Suddenly, from the parade, he heard a man shouting, "Watch the west wall! Watch the west wall!"

No sooner had the words died out in the air, than a dozen redskinned scalers came over the top of the wall. Some stopped to grapple with the five troopers who remained on the ramp. The others quickly dropped inside, bringing their rifles to bear. A wicked volley pursued, engulfing the parade in smoke.

Dan threw a quick glance eastward and saw that the Comanche ranks had thinned considerably. There were still eleven or twelve troopers firing from the east ramp, in addition to Lieutenant Puter, who was now using a carbine.

Flinging his legs over the edge of the wooden platform, Dan gripped the edge momentarily, then dropped to the ground. Gaining his balance, he wheeled, palming both Colts. He charged across the open area toward the Indians who had scaled the wall, guns blazing.

While reloading the carbine, Lieutenant Puter saw Dan wade into the scalers. Swinging off the wall, he drew his saber and his revolver and ran headlong across the parade toward the center of the battle.

Dan had dropped three Comanches, when he stumbled over a body in the smoke and fell to the ground. As he rolled in the dust, Puter charged past him, headed for a painted red warrior. Suddenly an arrow came from the west ramp, ripping into the lieutenant's chest. Colt caught sight of the Indian on the ramp and let both guns roar. The impact of the two .45 slugs knocked him backward. He sailed over the wall and disappeared.

Abruptly, the booming guns ceased firing inside the fort. Every scaler was dead. A few intermittent shots were fired from the wall, then silence prevailed.

"They're gone!" came a voice from the wall.

Dan holstered his guns and knelt beside Puter. The arrow was buried deep in his chest, just to the right of his heart. Blood trickled from both corners of his mouth. Opening his eyes, he tried to focus them on Dan's face. "Colt . . . I—" He coughed, spewing blood. "I—"

"Don't try to talk, lieutenant," said Dan. Pivoting

on his knees, he looked toward the spot where he had last seen Doc Springston. "Doc! Doc!"

A voice came from somewhere. "Doc's dead!"

Dan couldn't believe his ears. Turning back to the fallen lieutenant, he said, "We'll get the arrow out as soon as—"

"No need," cut in Puter. "I . . . know it's . . . it's . . ." His eyes glassed over. He coughed one more time and went limp.

Dan stood up and looked toward the place where Captain Radmacher had gone down. Two troopers were kneeling over him. As Dan approached, one lifted his eyes and said solemnly, "He's dead."

Suddenly, a familiar voice cut the air from the porch of the infirmary. Colonel Allen had been carried in a straight-backed chair and placed where he could issue orders. The two surviving lieutenants were hopping about like stringed puppets as Allen barked commands.

The impact of Doc Springston's death had not hit Dan until this minute. Without Doc, there was no proof for Logan Tanner . . . except for the affidavit. Doc had not brought it to him last night. Maybe he had left it up to Radmacher to deliver it. A cold wave of despair crept over him, followed by a sharp edge of panic.

Trying to appear as normal as possible, Dan crossed the sun-drenched parade. A trooper spoke up as he passed, "That was some fancy shooting when you came off that ramp, civilian." Dan smiled tightly, nodded, and kept moving.

The door to Captain Radmacher's quarters was unlocked. Dan slipped in, closing the door behind him.

His first move was to the rolltop desk. The top was down and locked. This is where the paper would be. He had to get into that desk.

Roaming the room with his eyes, he looked for something to pry loose the top. Nothing in sight. Rummaging through five dresser drawers produced nothing. In desperation, the tall man opened a closet door. There, hanging from a nail in a leather sheath, was a large hunting knife.

Quickly, Dan unsheathed the knife and crossed the room. Slipping the blade under the edge of the top, he bore down on the handle. The top gave some, but fell back into place as he released the pressure. He slid the blade closer to the lock and pried again. It made a slight popping noise. Hitting the knife handle with the heel of his hand to drive the blade deeper, Dan gave the knife a powerful upward jerk. The lock gave, scattering bits of wood and metal.

Rolling the top back, Dan sifted through some loose papers on the desk. Nothing. Nimbly, his fingers searched through every drawer, slot, and cubbyhole. Still nothing.

It seemed unlikely that Radmacher would bother to put the paper in his office desk, but that would be the next place to look.

Easing out the door onto the shaded porch, Dan walked casually toward the office area. From across the parade came a youthful voice. "Mister Colt! Mister Colt!" It was a private with a dusty uniform and a dirty face.

"Yes!" Dan answered.

"Colonel Allen wants to see you, Mister Colt."

Daniel Colt was in no mood to talk with the

abrasive colonel, but at this point, there was no escaping it. Stepping into the scorching sunlight, he ambled across the open area to where Allen sat on the infirmary porch.

"Ah, Colt," said the colonel. "With your medical know-how, I need you to help with the wounded. *The doctor is dead, you know.*"

There was an evil ring in that last statement. For the moment, Dan could do nothing but ignore it. "Yes, I know," said Dan.

"If you will help, it will free another man for burial detail. With this heat, we've got to get these bodies in the ground today."

"Sure, I'll help," said Dan, "but I'm no doctor."

"Just go in the infirmary. Tell the man who knows the least about what he's doing in there to come out and see me."

As Dan Colt ducked his head and entered the infirmary, Colonel Jeffrey Allen smiled to himself. The losses in this morning's battle were heavy and serious. Very unfortunate was the death of Doctor Springston. However, for the passion that burned in Allen's heart, things could not have worked out more perfectly.

Springston's death left only one witness for Marshal Logan Tanner—the affidavit. A warm sense of satisfaction flowed through the colonel. Dan Colt wanted that affidavit as much as Jeffrey Allen wanted Joe Caraway and his cohorts. There was no reason why they could not work out a deal. Caraway, Deere, Stevens, and Hopper . . . for the affidavit.

By late afternoon the wounded men were treated and made as comfortable as possible. A combined burial service for the twenty-three dead men was held at the Fort Ryan cemetery, a quarter-mile north of the walls. The wounded men sat in silence and listened as a twenty-one gun salute was offered, followed by the sound of taps.

The sun disappeared behind the distant mountains, setting the low-lying clouds afire and staining the New Mexico desert a blood red.

Dan Colt had formulated plans to get into Radmacher's office after dark. He ate his evening meal with the enlisted men. Talk was at a minimum. There were a few references to some incidents during the battle. The only other discussion centered around the dwindling ranks and how they were going to meet the Comanche onslaughts that were sure to come.

Excusing himself from the table, Dan stepped out into the night. A big yellow moon was peeking over the same wall where he had slaughtered Comanches that morning. The crickets were giving out their music. Somewhere in the distance a lone coyote yapped at the moon.

Dan was able to slip into Radmacher's office unnoticed. There was enough moonlight to see what he was doing, but thirty minutes of search produced no affidavit. His next inspection must be the infirmary. Doc must have had it, planning to give it to him this morning. Then the Comanches had come.

Searching the infirmary presented a real problem— Allen. He would probably stay there under Mrs. Herndon's care for several more days.

While crossing the parade, thinking on his problem, Dan wondered why trouble had an addiction for singling him out. Ever since Mary's brutal and senseless murder, everything in his life had turned sour. Well, *nearly* everything. He *had* escaped Yuma Prison by a stroke of good fortune. He *was* able to track down and kill Mary's murderers. But now, just when it seemed this long nightmare of bearing Dave's crimes was over, his star witness is killed by Comanches. The last, thin thread of hope was to find that affidavit.

Colonel Jeffrey Allen was sitting on the infirmary porch, enjoying the cool evening breeze. Dan made up his mind he would flat out tell the man why he wanted to search the infirmary. He was within thirty yards of where the colonel sat when a rifle barked from the east wall.

Dan whirled as a second gun sounded, followed by a wild yell outside the wall. There was a mad scramble among the troopers.

"Comanches!" came an excited voice.

A volley of shots was fired as Dan bounded to the ladder and landed on the ramp with both guns drawn. Just as he peered over the wall, the troopers stopped shooting.

"Tryin' to pick up their dead," observed one of the troopers. "Now there's some more to pick up."

Dan's eyes swept the moonlit flats. Inert forms of scattered bodies dotted the area.

"They'll keep comin' till they've gathered their dead warriors," said another.

"And I'll keep killin' 'em," replied the first one.

The long-bodied Colt descended the ladder and headed for the infirmary. Both lieutenants were in conversation with the colonel. As Dan approached,

Allen said, "The savages will not give up, Colt, until they've cleared the field."

"Guess not," Dan said idly.

"Colt," said the colonel, "have you met these two officers?"

"I've seen them, but not met them," said Dan, offering his hand to the closer one. "Dan Colt."

"Gerald Fleming," said the young lieutenant.

Reaching across Fleming, Dan gripped the hand of the other one, who said, "Bill Stark."

"We'll talk it over in the morning, colonel," said Fleming. "I doubt the red devils will attack again for a couple of days."

Both men saluted. Allen returned it from his seated position and watched as both men strode away in the silver light.

"I want to take a look in the infirmary," said Dan, getting right to the point. "I'm trying to find the affidavit Doc signed for me."

A look of gilded triumph claimed Allen's face. Dan could see it clearly in the moonlight. A cold dread in Dan's stomach prophesied what he was about to hear.

"You won't find it," said Allen evenly. "I have it."

Dan stared at the man, straightening to his full height. He stood tall and severe, his face a mask of granite, anger gradually possessing him. When he spoke, there was ice in his voice. "I don't have to ask why."

"You can have the affidavit, gunhawk, when you bring in Joe Caraway and his three pals." There was a tone of finality in the colonel's voice. He had Dan over the proverbial barrel and both men knew it. "You can light out in the morning. My offer still stands. I'll get you top money from the government, plus my two thousand."

"You really want 'em bad, don't you?"

"How bad you want that affidavit?" asked Allen, raising his heavy eyebrows.

"Blood and guts bad," rasped Colt, thin-lipped. "That's how bad I want those filthy deserters."

"So it's a Mexican standoff," Dan breathed hotly.

"*Si, senor*," grinned the colonel.

"What happens when Tanner shows up here?"

"I'll tell him you're on an errand for me and you'll be back soon."

"You'll not show him the paper?"

"I thought you wanted that pleasure for yourself."

"I do," said Dan, "but if he starts to leave, you give it to him."

"No," said Allen curtly, "we'll do that when you get back."

"But I could be gone weeks... maybe months!"

"If Tanner wants you as bad as you say, he'll wait right here when I tell him you're going to ride through the gate just any day."

"He'll only wait so long, Allen, and you know it." Dan's blood coursed his veins like bubbling lava.

An opulent grin crept over Allen's deeply lined face. "Then that will be your incentive to work fast, won't it, my boy?"

CHAPTER ELEVEN

The four army-issue Colt .44's dropped to the carpet of pine needles, each making a soft, muffled sound.

Dave Sundeen's jaw clenched hard as he fixed his ice-blue stare on the quartet before him, hands over their heads. Towering tall and formidable on the boulder, he said, "Now, what are you soldier boys doing way up here in the mountains? The Indians are down on the desert."

Easing his hands down, Joe Caraway said, "We got off the trail—"

"Get those hands back up!" barked Sundeen. "Now, I can hold these twins in this position a lot longer than you can keep your hands in the air. I want the truth and you're gonna stay that way till I get it."

"Just as well go ahead and tell him, Joe," advised Frank Stevens. "This feller ain't no fool."

Caraway dropped his chin, cleared his throat, then

raised his eyes to meet those of the man behind the Colt .45's. Shifting his feet slightly, but keeping his arms erect, he said, "We know you robbed the Burlington stage yesterday. Got away with a cash box with thirty-five hundred dollars."

"The cavalry doesn't chase bandits, sergeant," Sundeen said flatly, suspicion written on his angular face.

"We ain't cavalry," responded Caraway.

"Stole the uniforms, eh?"

"Uh . . . not exactly," said Caraway. "We're ... uh ... deserters."

"When, how, and why'd you do it?" asked Sundeen, his face shaping into an impassive mold.

"Few days ago," answered the man with three chevrons on his sleeve. "South of Socorro a ways."

"Look, mister, our arms are getting tired," butted in Ken Deere. "Can't we put our hands down?"

"If you want daylight in your belly," replied the tall man coldly. Dave shifted his stare back to Caraway for the rest of the story.

"We didn't hurt anybody," Caraway lied. "Just rode away from a patrol."

"The others didn't shoot at you?"

"Uh . . . no. We *snuck* away at night," Joe lied again.

"Why?"

"Decided there was too much risk for too little pay."

"I won't disagree with that," said Sundeen.

Alex Hopper bit his lip and lowered his aching arms. Sundeen's left-hand .45 roared. The bullet ripped through Hopper's shirt-sleeve just under the armpit. Eyes bulging, he snapped his arms upward.

"Next time I'll cut the tip off your elbow, son," Dave said coolly. Looking back at the sergeant, he said, "So you were gonna rob me of my loot, eh?"

Caraway's face flushed to match the color of the sky to the east. "Yes, sir."

"You were ready for us," said Frank Stevens. "How did you know—"

"It was the cougar," Hopper hurried to answer.

"No. It was the monkey," said Sundeen.

"Monkey?" asked Caraway.

"The one on the pole yesterday. Which one of you was it?"

"Me," replied Ken Deere, face reddened.

"I watched you clods ride up the mountain on my trail," said Dave. "Rode down here and built a fire for you."

The four deserters looked at each other resignedly.

"If you four are going in the man-tracking business, you better bone up a little," advised Sundeen.

"We're not," said Joe, "but we are in the holdup business. Same as you. We knocked off both banks in Socorro yesterday. These uniforms really catch people off guard."

Sundeen pursed his lips and nodded. "Good thinking," he said with a note of admiration.

Caraway ran his eyes to the faces of the other three, then fixed his gaze on Sundeen. "Look, mister—"

"Sundeen. Dave Sundeen," the man with the twin Colts said evenly.

"Look, Mister Sundeen," continued Caraway, "we were just talkin' yesterday how we need a fifth man. Most patrols are five or more. Would help ease any suspicion if we had another man. Not only that, but it would help when we hit a bank. Speed things up when we're inside."

"It won't last long. Word'll get out," said Sundeen.

"We know that," replied Caraway, "but we can clean up good for about three or four weeks. Shake the uniforms, pack our riches, and get outta this part of the country."

"Couple of problems," said Dave. "Cavalrymen don't ride buckskins. They ride bays with government brands on their hips . . . McClellan saddles . . . regulation Colt .44 sidearms . . . blue uniforms with yellow stripes on the trousers . . . Castellani sabers."

"We'll find a way to get into Fort Clayton, over by Albuquerque," said Caraway. "We'll get you outfitted. You can leave your horse with one of the hostlers in Albuquerque . . . come back and get him when we have to quit business."

Alex Hopper was in agony. He looked like he was going to pass out.

"Okay, men," said Dave, "you can drop your arms."

All four sighed and responded.

"If one of you tries to pick up a gun before I tell him, he's a dead man," warned Sundeen.

The men in blue rubbed their aching shoulders.

"What are your names?" asked the tall, blue-eyed man.

"I'm Joe Caraway," said the sergeant.

"Alex Hopper."

"Frank Stevens."

"Ken Deere."

"I take it you're the leader," Sundeen said to Caraway.

Caraway nodded.

"Nobody bosses me. Understood?" rasped Sundeen.

Caraway nodded again.

"We split everything equal?" asked Dave.

"It's the way we've been doin' it," answered the sergeant.

"Best that way," said Sundeen. "That way nobody gets to feelin' sorry for himself."

All nodded in agreement.

"We start as of now, right? Previous jobs not included."

"Sure enough, Mister Sundeen," put in Ken Deere. "We wouldn't try to horn in on the thirty-five hundred you got in the cash box yesterday."

"You'd have a tough time doin' that," said Dave. The four men eyed him carefully. "I buried it somewhere in these mountains. The map's in my head."

Joe Caraway chuckled. Deere followed suit, then Hopper. Finally, all five laughed heartily together.

"Well," said Sundeen, "now that everything's settled, you holster your guns, bring in your horses, and let's have breakfast."

Thirty minutes later, the five bandits made plans over hot coffee and cold rations. Albuquerque's three banks were situated far enough apart. They would rob all three day after tomorrow. The next two days would be spent getting Dave Sundeen outfitted and ready for his role as a U.S. cavalry trooper.

Ken Deere volunteered to ride into Fort Clayton. He would tell them a special unit from Fort Ryan was camped out on the desert. Comanches had attacked them, killed one horse, and kidnapped a trooper. He would give a wild tale about how the rest of the unit stormed the Comanche camp and rescued the trooper, who had been stripped of his clothing. He would need to be entirely outfitted, including horse and saddle. All would be returned once the unit could make it back to Fort Ryan.

"There's no way they can verify the unit," chuckled Deere. "The lines are down between the forts." Looking at Dave, Deere said, "Write down your measurements and boot size, Mister Sundeen. Hat size, too. I'll fit you as close as possible."

"You can call me *Dave*," said the tall man, touching each face with his gaze. Producing paper and a stub pencil, he scribbled for a moment and handed the paper to Deere.

Speaking to Ken Deere, Caraway said, "You go ahead and ride to the fort. We'll wait for you here. Be sure to circle out onto the desert and approach the fort from the west. You'll have to leave the same way. It'll take the better part of today for you to make the trip."

Deere nodded and mounted his horse. As he reined the animal around, Caraway said, "Ken..."

"Yeah," responded Deere.

"Better get some ammunition, too. Tell 'em we are runnin' low."

"You bet," said the mounted man and rode away.

The rest of the day at the camp was spent formulating plans for bank and stagecoach robberies. Dave Sundeen was a little uncomfortable. He usually worked alone. He pacified himself, however, with the knowledge that this setup would be short-lived. The idea of traveling and robbing in cavalry uniforms was excellent. He should have enough cash when this stint was over to last a long while.

Deep inside of Dave Sundeen was a distaste for robbing, but there was no other way to make a living. He had tried, on several occasions, to settle down and take a job. Usually it was as a ranch hand. But sooner or later, his past would crop up and he would be on the move again. He had done well gambling at times, but so often the poker games ended in gunsmoke and bloodshed.

He made good as a bounty hunter for a while, but with his own reputation, he was more often the hunted than the hunter. Hence, Dave Sundeen was like a man riding a tiger. If you get off, you're a dead man. Robbing banks and stagecoaches was his means of existence.

The robberies held for the tall, blond man, one haunting dread—the chance that he would have to kill someone during a robbery. He had no problem killing a man in a stand-up fast-draw. In Dave's gunfighting career, he had always been the challenged, not the challenger. If a man challenged him and died in the shootout, *tough*. He asked for it. But in a robbery, Dave Sundeen was the initiator. It was natural for the victims to fight back. In thirty or more robberies, he had not killed anyone. He had winged a few . . . like the shotgunner on the Burlington stage yesterday . . . but so far, no one had been killed.

With this dread riding high in his mind, Sundeen said to Joe Caraway, "There's one more thing we need to discuss."

"What's that, Dave?"

Sundeen let his gaze move slowly from face to face among the three men. "I don't want any unnecessary killing."

The men in blue eyed each other.

"I know when we put guns on people, they are apt to get brave. Or foolish. If we should have to shoot them, okay, but we don't need to try to kill them."

Frank Stevens spoke up. "You didn't hesitate to bore a hole in that shotgunner yesterday."

Sundeen's frosty-blue eyes fixed themselves on Stevens's face. "Was he alive when you saw him?"

"Well, I . . . uh . . . really d-didn't get much of a l-look at him," stammered Stevens. "He was inside the coach. I—"

"Was he alive?" bit in Sundeen.

"Yes."

"If he was alive, it was because I meant for him to be alive," said Dave coldly. "I had to shoot him. I told him to drop the shotgun. He swung it on me. I put a slug in his arm."

"Bet he dropped it then," chuckled Alex Hopper nervously.

The other two joined for a forced bit of laughter.

Knowing he had put the men on edge, Dave said, "All I'm sayin', fellas, is no unnecessary killing, okay?"

"Sure. Sure, Dave," said Joe Caraway. "We all feel the same way, don't we, fellas?"

"Yeah. Right," agreed Stevens.

"We haven't killed nobody so far," lied Caraway. "We aim to keep it that way, if possible."

The day wore on. The sun had already disappeared behind the rugged peaks to the west, when the muffled sound of hooves on pine needles sifted through the forest. The four men in the camp were instantly on their feet, guns in hand. For several moments they peered into the dark shadows. Presently, Ken Deere emerged into the clearing, leading a bay gelding bearing the U.S. brand on its hip. A large canvas bag was tied to the McClellan saddle.

Deere smiled as the robbers holstered their guns. Slipping from the saddle, he said, "Evenin', boys."

"They bought your story, I take it," said Joe Caraway.

"Like it was gold going for five dollars an ounce," chuckled Deere. Throwing a glance at Sundeen, he said, "Horse look all right to you?"

"No complaints," answered Dave.

Stepping to the canvas bag, Deere released it from the saddle. "Think I got you outfitted to a 'T,' Dave," he said with a smile.

While Alex Hopper built a fire, Ken Deere laid out Dave's uniform, including hat and boots. Sundeen removed his own flat-crowned hat and replaced it with the gray hat bearing the gold-colored cross sabers. "Perfect fit," he observed audibly.

Picking up the black military boots, Sundeen walked to a fallen tree and sat down. While he was trying them for size, Joe Caraway asked Deere, "They ask questions?"

"Nope. Only if we needed help. I told them that with the horse and the rest of this we'd be all right."

"You get cartridges?"

"Uh-huh. Five boxes."

"Good."

Dave Sundeen's voice came from where the uniform was laid out. "Guess I outrank you, now, Caraway." He was holding a coat and a shirt with lieutenant's bars attached.

Caraway's eyes bolted Ken Deere.

"He's a big man, Joe," said Deere defensively. "Supply man asked the trooper's rank. I told him *corporal*. There was nobody around to sew on the stripes, so he pinned on the bars. Said it wouldn't make any difference anyhow, since we were just headin' back to Ryan. Said he couldn't let the uniform out without a rank. None of the clothes with stripes already sewed on were big enough."

"Don't let it worry you, Joe," laughed Sundeen, "I won't boss you in front of anybody."

Plans were finalized for the next day. Dave Sundeen would ride into Albuquerque while the others waited outside of town. He would make a slow tour, checking each of the three banks. This done, he would take the big buckskin to the hostler, leaving him to board. He would walk to the edge of town, where the four men in blue would meet him with the army horse. They would withdraw for the rest of the day to a secluded spot and camp for the night. The banks opened at ten o'clock. They would hit the first one the moment it opened.

With the fire burning brightly, the five men bedded down for the night. The wind played a mournful tune in the trees. The horses stood in silence, sniffing the wind, while the dancing flames threw flickering shadows on their shiny coats.

Hours passed. The fire dwindled to a few red embers, brightened at times by gusts of wind.

The big buckskin gelding was the first to alert the

campers. He ejected a loud, drawn-out whinny and pounded the earth with his forelegs.

Dave Sundeen was instantly awake. He bounded to his feet as the other horses fought the ropes that held them to the trees. Dave blinked against the darkness, running his sleepy eyes in a panorama around the campfire.

The other men were scrambling to their feet now. Joe Caraway ordered Alex Hopper to build up the fire. Suddenly, from the darkness came the vicious hiss of a cougar, followed by a deep-throated growl. The growl grew in volume.

Pointing past the big rock where Dave Sundeen had first appeared to the men in blue, Frank Stevens said, "He's right back there!"

Each man fixed his eyes in the direction Stevens was pointing, levering his carbine for action. The roar came again, threatening, vicious. The fire came alive, giving light against the perimeter of the clearing. The eyes of the horses were white and wild.

Still, the cat had not appeared. Again, a high-pitched warning came from the darkness, from the same direction.

Alex Hopper threw the rifle to his shoulder.

"Wait!" cried Dave Sundeen. "Don't shoot till you can see what you're shooting at!"

"I know he's out there!" retaliated Hopper.

"You wouldn't hit that cat in a million years pot-shotting the dark," snapped Sundeen. "Put more wood on the fire." Speaking to the others, who stood frozen in their tracks, he said, "Each of you pick up a burning stick and wave it slowly. Walk toward the horses. The cat is after the h—"

BANDITS IN BLUE

Suddenly, the cougar charged past the big rock, headed in a straight line for the horses. The frightened animals screamed. Dave raised his rifle and fired at the brown streak. Two more shots were fired. The cat let out a mortal cry, staggered a few steps, and collapsed on its side.

The dead cougar lay at the edge of the firelight. As the five men approached it, Frank Stevens said, "You think it's the one we threw rocks at last night?"

"Hard to tell," said Joe Caraway. "They all look pretty much alike."

Ken Deere swore. "He's a biggy. I'd sure hate to face him comin' at me head-on!"

"Cat like that can kill a man with one blow," said Joe.

The horses were still unsettled. Stevens walked toward them, speaking soothingly. The others turned toward the fire.

"You'd think the horses would calm down, now that that blood-curdlin' roar has stopped," said Hopper, easing his rifle to the ground.

The buckskin whinnied shrilly again.

Looking toward Stevens and the horses, Sundeen said, "Trouble with these cats . . . sometimes they travel in pairs. You have to be—"

From out of the darkness a cougar appeared, charging directly toward Ken Deere, who was farthest from the fire. Deere had laid down the carbine and was kneeling beside his saddle. The frenzied beast was coming from the opposite side of the circle from where the horses were tied.

Dave saw the cat's eyes flash in the dark. It was bearing down on Deere with unbelievable speed. For

Sundeen, it would be a head-on shot. There was no time to bring the rifle to bear and lever in a cartridge.

Caraway screamed, "*Ken!*"

Deere looked up, staring into the oncoming eyes of the cat. Before Dave Sundeen's carbine struck earth, the twin Colt .45's leaped into his hands and roared. Both bullets centered the cougar's head. The charging beast went down in a ball of rolling fur, slamming into Deere and knocking him flat.

Quickly, the frightened man scrambled out from underneath the dead cat. His eyes were wide. Shaking himself, he said, "Th-thanks, Dave. I would have been a goner!"

Alex Hopper looked Sundeen up and down, mouth gaping. "I ain't never seen such shootin' in all my precious life. Remind me to never brace you in a gunfight!"

CHAPTER TWELVE

The four deserters watched Dave Sundeen ride away from the cottonwood grove a mile south of Albuquerque's outskirts. The sun was midway in the morning sky.

A Wells Fargo stage raised a cloud of dust as it pulled out of town heading for Socorro.

"Maybe we oughtta intercept that stage while Dave's makin' his tour of town," Ken Deere said to Joe Caraway.

"We'll wait right here," said Caraway. "There'll be plenty of stages to stop after today. With Sundeen along we got a lot better chance of success."

Dave Sundeen rode into Albuquerque, his gaze moving slowly from left to right. The first three blocks were adobe houses, most of them unprotected from the grueling rays of the sun. A few rested beneath cottonwoods and willows.

In the first block of business section, the tall rider

spied the Rio Grande Corral. There was a weather-worn sign that advertised, among other things, HORSES BOARDED. "That'll be your hotel, boy," Sundeen said to the big buckskin underneath him.

There followed the usual disconnected double line of sun-bleached frame buildings, topped by a facade of false fronts. On the southwest corner of the second block stood the Albuquerque Bank and Trust. Dave eyed it carefully as he rode by. He saw nothing that should hinder a clean and simple getaway.

Moving further up the dusty street, he passed several saloons. One, he noted, had just built on a new wing and installed a big gambling place like those in San Francisco. A freshly painted sign called it the Blue Chip Casino. Dave could hear laughter coming from within.

Four blocks from the first bank was number two, the Bank of New Mexico. Dave did a quick second look when he saw that the sheriff's office was directly across the street from the bank. *This will take a little extra work*, he told himself. Warily, he eyed the barred windows on the jail. The thought of being locked up was a repugnant one.

The business establishments continued three more blocks. The First National Bank was in the center of the last block. From that point, the town stretched north for four more. Dave noticed that new houses were being built in the last block.

The big buckskin made a wide circle in the street and headed back. Dave Sundeen's only concern was the Bank of New Mexico. He did not like the position of that sheriff's office.

Dismounting in front of the general store, Dave

went inside. A few moments later he emerged, carrying a flat brown paper sack. Placing it in a saddlebag, he mounted the buckskin once again.

Moving slowly down the street, he saw that a crowd had gathered in front of the Blue Chip Casino. They were circled around two men, who were cursing each other heatedly. Dave swung his leg over the saddle and tied the buckskin to the hitchrail across the street. Slowly he crossed the street and stood on the edge of the crowd.

One man was young, mean-looking. His Frontier Colt .44 was hung low and thonged to his leg.

The other man was well into his fifties and bore no resemblance to a gunfighter. He wore a sidearm, but in no position for a fast draw. Dave figured he was a cowhand from some local ranch.

As the argument continued, a middle-aged man standing next to Sundeen said, "Know who that young gunslick is, mister?"

"Nope," said Dave with obvious lack of interest.

"That's 'Bad Boy' Bobby Braden!"

"Oh."

"Faster'n a hummin' bird's stroke and meaner'n a bloated bull!"

"Oh. Who's that other fella?"

"That's Doak Wood. Cowpuncher at the S-Bar-S north o' here."

"What's the friction over?" asked Sundeen.

"Poker game. Doak caught 'Bad Boy' cheatin'. Least he's sayin' he did."

Braden's voice pierced the air. "Are you callin' me a liar, cowboy?"

"Put your own tag on it, Braden," retorted the

puncher. "You and I both know you pulled that card from your shirt-sleeve. I want my part of the pot back."

The lean-bodied Braden backed up, bumping the people standing behind him. His right hand hung over the butt of his gun, fingers curled like deathly talons. "There's only one way you'll get money offa me, horse-fuzz. That's when I'm layin' right there in the dust."

The crowd began to withdraw, breaking the circle. Dave looked into the older man's wind-checked face. Fear glazed his eyes.

"I'm not wantin' no shootout, Braden," said Wood shakily. "I just want my money back. You cheated me."

Braden stood, shoulders hunched, feet spread apart. His face was cold and impassive. "I told you how to get it," he said through his teeth.

"Why doesn't somebody do something?" came a woman's voice. "He's going to kill that cowboy."

"Not unless Wood draws on him," said an unidentified man.

Braden spit out the side of his mouth, eyes fixed on Wood.

"Look," said Wood, raising his hands in a feeble gesture, "I ain't no gunf—"

Braden's taloned hand drew and fired with lightning speed. The bullet tore into the cowpuncher's chest, the impact flattening him on the ground. The crowd stood in stunned silence. One man spoke, as Dave Sundeen moved forward and knelt beside Doak Wood. "He wasn't drawin' on you, Braden . . . and you know it!"

"Bad Boy" Bobby Braden casually blew smoke from his .44 muzzle, broke the action, punched out the empty shell, and replaced it. "He moved his hands," said Braden coldly, easing the gun in the holster. "I thought he was goin' for his gun."

Deeply engraved in Dave Sundeen's outlaw heart was an unshakable distaste for cocky, cold-blooded killers. They were like overbearing, ferocious jungle beasts, preying on the weak and feeble. As he removed the hat of the dead man and placed it over the pallid face, he stood up and eyed the insolent killer. Braden's gaze lined up with the frosty-blue eyes of Sundeen. After a few seconds, "Bad Boy" let his eyes drop to the low-slung twin Colts.

Sundeen's face hardened. His eyes narrowed. "Did you cheat this man?"

Braden started to speak. Before his words could form, a heavyset man wearing a black suit cut in, "He sure did, Mister Colt. I was at the table. Saw it with my own eyes."

Braden threw the man a hot glare.

"I asked you a question," said Dave sternly. He held Braden with his icy stare.

"He did, Mister Colt," repeated the man in the black suit.

"I don't have to tell you nuthin'," snapped "Bad Boy."

"Braden, you're a fool," said the man in the black suit. "Don't you know who you're talkin' to?"

"You called him 'Mister Colt,' fat man," iced Braden. Fixing his mouth in a smirk, he looked at Dave. "Colt, huh? Is that as in *gun* . . . or *horse*?"

The man in black said emphatically, "That's *Dan* Colt, 'Bad Boy'!"

Holding his gaze on Braden, Dave said, "You're mistaken about that, mister—"

"Uh... Henry Byas, Mister Colt."

"You're mistaken, Mister Byas. My name's David Sundeen. I've heard of Dan Colt, but I'm not him."

"I'm from Kansas, Colt," said Byas heavily. "I've seen you plenty of times. Couldn't be two of you look that much alike."

"I've never seen him," said Sundeen, "so I can't comment on that. Hear he's like a well-oiled machine when he draws."

The smirk on Bobby Braden's face twisted into an insolent sneer. "Maybe you're coverin' up, Colt, because you're gettin' old. Hmm? Maybe you've outlived your reputation."

"I'm not Dan Colt," insisted Dave.

"Seems this fat man is mighty sure you *are*," snapped Bobby. "But you've heard of 'Bad Boy' Braden and your draw has slowed. You've developed a yellow streak down your back. You're afraid—"

"Don't flatter yourself, punk," cut in Sundeen, a raw edge to his voice. "I've never heard of you. And what's more, you're kiddin' yourself if you think you're in Dan Colt's league. He could blow you away in his sleep."

"You think I'll walk away and not make you draw if you convince me you're not Colt. Is that it?" Braden's hand eased slowly over the gun butt, once again curling his fingers as deathly talons. "You're not gettin' out of this one, Mister Dan Colt. It's time to move aside for 'Bad Boy' Braden."

Flame flicked at Sundeen's insides. The crowd stood in awe. Dave spoke coldly, emphasizing every word. "My name is Dave Sundeen. Just want you to know it before you die. Draw, punk."

Braden's hand darted downward. Sundeen's .45's roared in one death-dealing staccato. "Bad Boy" was dead before he hit the street. His fingers were frozen tight on the butt of the gun, which was still in its holster.

As blue smoke drifted skyward, Dave holstered the Colts. Running his gaze over the wide-eyed crowd, he said, "Did the cowhand have a wife?"

"Yessir, Mister Colt," came a reply from the crowd. "She lives at the S-Bar-S."

Kneeling beside Braden's lifeless form, Dave rifled his pockets, producing a roll of bills. Standing up, he said, "Is there a lawman in this town?"

"Sheriff's up in Santa Fe," came a man's voice. "Deputy is deliverin' some legal papers to a ranch a few miles west."

"You wantin' to be sure that money gets to Doak's widow, Mister Colt?" asked Henry Byas.

"That's it."

"I'm president of the First National Bank. Would you trust me to deliver it?"

"Sure. Give her the whole roll," said Dave, extending it to the fat man. As Byas took it, Dave looked him in the eye. "And Mister Byas . . ."

"Yes?"

"My name is not Dan Colt." With that, Sundeen crossed the street, swung into the saddle, and rode away.

Henry Byas stood, hat tilted, scratching his head.

Morgan Hill

As Dave Sundeen trotted the gelding toward the south end of town, he was pondering the banker's mistake in identity. Suddenly he remembered that somewhere not long ago, someone else had made the same mistake. *Can't remember who or where that was*, he thought to himself, *but somebody took me for Dan Colt.*

"Here he comes," Alex Hopper advised the others. Caraway, Deere, and Stevens were stretched out on the ground, in the shade. Hopper leaned against a cottonwood, eyes glued to the road. The prostrate three rose to their feet and watched Sundeen ride in.

"Heard some shootin'," said Caraway, as Dave dismounted. "You in on that?"

"Yep," replied the tall man. "Gunslick took out a thick-fingered cowboy. Then decided to try me on for size."

"Guess we don't have to ask who won," said Stevens idly.

"Take a mighty good man to outdraw you," said Hopper, eyes wide with admiration. "I bet you'd be a good match for Bat Masterson, Wyatt Earp, . . . or Dan Colt."

Sundeen's head snapped around. *"Dan Colt?"*

"Yeah," said Alex Hopper.

"Why'd you mention Dan Colt?" Sundeen's eyes were fixed on those of Alex Hopper.

"Well . . . 'cause he is heat-lightnin' fast," said Hopper, blinking.

"You ever seen this Dan Colt?"

"Uh . . . no. No," said Hopper, nervous under Sundeen's glare. "But I've heard a lot."

Sundeen tilted his flat-crowned hat to the back of his head. "Ever heard anybody describe him?"

"Plenty," answered Hopper. "They say he has pale blue eyes that look right through—" Alex swallowed hard. "That look right through you. Like—uh . . . like *yours*."

"How's he built?" asked Dave.

"They say he's tall—uh . . . blond—uh . . . like—"

"Like *me*?"

"Uh . . . yeah. Yeah. L-like you."

Joe Caraway spoke up. "Hey, Dave. You're not—"

"No," snapped Sundeen. "But twice lately I've been mistaken for him by people who've seen him. The second one was a few minutes ago by a big thick-bodied banker."

"Seems I heard somethin' about this Colt gunhawk bein' ambushed a few years back," put in Frank Stevens. "Buried somewhere out on the Kansas plains."

"I heard that, too," said Ken Deere. "But then I also heard that he was seen up in Colorado and over in Utah not long ago."

"Must be a mighty strong resemblance 'tween you two," said Stevens.

"One other thing, too," added Alex Hopper. "They tell me he wears a pair o' twin Colts, just like you, Dave."

"Hmmm," said Sundeen. "Maybe someday I'll get a chance to meet this Colt dude."

"That'd be interesting," said Hopper.

Changing the subject, Dave Sundeen ran his gaze across the four faces and said, "Boys, we gotta do a little extra figurin' with the number two bank."

"Which one's that?" asked Joe Caraway.

"The Bank of New Mexico," replied Sundeen. "Bernalillo County sheriff's office is smack dab across the street."

Caraway swore. "Maybe we oughtta just pass it by."

"No way," said Dave. "We'll just have to handle things first."

"Whaddya mean?" asked Ken Deere.

"I found out at the shootin' ruckus today that the sheriff is in Santa Fe. Apparently there's only one deputy. He was out of town servin' some papers. No doubt he'll be around tomorrow."

"When's the sheriff comin' back?" asked Caraway.

"I don't know," replied Sundeen, "but I'll talk to the deputy first thing in the morning. Find out. Then put the deputy out of commission."

"What if the sheriff's already back, or expected back real soon?" queried Caraway.

"Then we'll hold off and go for it the next mornin' after we've put both lawmen out of commission," replied Sundeen flatly.

"Why do we have to put it off another day?" asked Alex Hopper. "Why can't we just wait till the sheriff shows ... cold-cock him and then hit the banks?"

"I thought I made it clear, Alex," said Sundeen. "If we're goin' to take three banks in one sweep, we've got to catch the first one right at opening time. Gotta stick the sign in the window. We don't dare have some customer get suspicious and holler 'bank robbery' while we're workin' on the other two."

"Oh. Sorry," said Hopper, dipping his chin. "I wasn't thinkin'."

"Did you get the pencil and paper?" asked Deere.

"Yep," answered Sundeen. Wheeling, he stepped to the saddlebag on the buckskin's back and pulled out the flat paper sack. "Might as well go ahead and make the sign." Pulling out a sheet of paper and a thick-leaded pencil, he sat down on a large rock and laid the sack on his lap. Placing the paper on the sack, he began printing large letters very carefully.

While Dave worked on the sign, Joe Caraway said, "If some of the people who saw you today see you walk into the sheriff's office in the morning in a blue uniform, won't they get suspicious? Maybe a couple of us ought to take care of the deputy."

"Rather handle it myself," replied Sundeen without looking up. "That's why I said *first thing* in the morning. Banks don't open till ten. Deputy will be at the office around eight. I'll take care of him, then leave my horse at the stable. One of you can meet me at the edge of town with my other horse."

Standing up as Caraway nodded in agreement, Dave held up the sign for all to see. In clear, dark letters, it read:

DUE TO UNEXPECTED INTERNAL PROBLEM,
BANK WILL NOT OPEN UNTIL TEN-THIRTY.
WE REGRET THIS INCONVENIENCE.

"Truer words were never written," chuckled Caraway.

"It *will* be unexpected," agreed Stevens, smiling broadly.

"Yeah," added Alex Hopper. "It'll be the worst kind of internal problem, too." He laughed heartily.

Morgan Hill

"They will also regret the inconvenience," chimed in Ken Deere. "They will regret it a whole lot!"

The five men laughed together.

The day passed slowly and finally night fell. Dave Sundeen and his new-found friends chatted idly over a supper of beans, hardtack, jerky, and coffee. The stars twinkled overhead. Soon the moon made its grand entrance, paling the stars in the eastern sky.

As the campfire dwindled, Dave lay awake listening to the others snore. His thoughts drifted back to the day's earlier conversation . . . to the insistence of Henry Byas that he was Dan Colt. *Dan Colt, the famous gunfighter. Some say he has killed over a hundred men. Most of them died trying to make a name for themselves.* Sundeen chuckled softly. *They did,* he thought. *On a grave marker in some Boot Hill.*

As his eyes grew heavy, Dave Sundeen had one last sleepy thought. *I wonder just how much we are alike . . .*

CHAPTER THIRTEEN

A fringe of pink was spreading along the eastern horizon as Dan Colt swung the saddle onto the broad back of his black gelding. He cast a glance at the troopers on the ramps of the four stockade walls, who vigilantly studied the desert for signs of movement. Colt knew that if the Comanches did not attack the fort by sunup, it would be safe for him to ride for Socorro.

He let the gelding take a long drink at the water trough, then led him to where Colonel Jeffrey Allen sat on the porch of the infirmary.

A look of conquest rode Allen's deeply lined face as Dan halted the horse where he sat. "You don't want to dillydally, Colt," said the colonel. "I'll detain your U.S. marshal friend as long as possible, but if you're gone too long, he just might decide to ride on."

"It won't be a problem if you'll just give him that affidavit," said Dan bitingly.

"Nope," retaliated Allen, grinning with triumph. "The only time I'll release that paper is when you ride in here with Caraway, Deere, Stevens, and Hopper—dead or alive."

Dan eyed the sunrise. Swinging lithely into the saddle, he set his ice-blue gaze on the colonel. Though the tall man's eyes were cold, they possessed a spark of fire from which Allen could not look away. Holding him there for a long moment, Dan spoke. His voice was like the hiss of a whip. "You'll get your pound of flesh, colonel, but if you let Tanner ride out of here before I get back, you're going to be one sorry son. Do I make myself clear?"

Allen swore. "How am I gonna hold him if he takes a mind to go?"

Colt's lips were drawn in a thin, petulant line. "You're the one that set the rules for this game, mister. All I can say is, you'd better keep him here. Got it?"

Allen nodded, a hint of vexation in his eyes. Dan touched the gelding's sides with his spurs. The colonel watched as he rode to the gate. He heard the sentry tell Colt that all was clear. The giant gate swung open. Horse and rider disappeared.

The flaming rim of the sun illuminated the desert as Dan Colt rode away from Fort Ryan. Taking up the trail, he rode the east bank of the Rio Grande toward Socorro. The deserters had headed north when they rode away. Maybe they had continued in that direction. He had to start somewhere. Socorro was as good a place as any.

The lazy town of Socorro was just coming to life as

the black gelding carried his tall, blond rider down the dusty main street. An old yellow dog sat in the middle of the street, slugglishly scratching his rib cage.

Reining in at the marshal's office, Colt dismounted and approached the door. It was locked. Leaning close to the window, he peered inside, seeking some sign of life. Suddenly from behind, a voice said, "Marshal ain't in, mister."

Wheeling around, Dan spied an elderly man standing in the inch-deep dust of the street. "What time does he come to the office?" queried the tall man.

"He ain't never comin' in again," said the old man flatly. "Marshal Travers is dead."

"Oh, I'm sorry," said Dan. "Killed?"

"Yep. In the line of duty. Bank robbers."

An unexplained something touched the base of Dan's spine. "Bank robbers?"

"Yep," replied the old gentleman. "They robbed both banks, one right after the other. Killed the marshal and Stanley Humm, the owner of our newspaper."

"When did this happen?" Colt asked quickly.

"Uh . . . 'bout five, six days ago. Queer thing about it, too."

"How's that?"

"They was U.S. army. Cavalrymen."

"Did you see 'em?" asked Dan, excitement building within him.

"Shore did," said the old man, nodding. "I was standin' right over there in front of Bailey's Hardware when the shootin' started. They come ridin' right by me. Killed a rancher who tried to stop 'em, too!"

"How many were there?"

"Four of 'em." Tilting his head, the old timer said, "You a lawman, sonny?"

"Uh ... no. No, I'm not."

"What'd you want to see the marshal about?"

"Oh, just some business," said Dan evasively. "Who's in charge of things since the marshal's dead?"

"Most likely be Luke Lemmon," said the old man, squinting against the light of the sun. "Luke is chairman of the town council." Pointing up the street, he said, "He runs the general store up there."

"Appreciate the information, friend," said Dan mounting the black.

"Yer downright welcome, young feller. Say, whut's yer name?"

"Dan Colt."

The old man laughed as horse and rider started up the street. "Yeah!" he said with a doubtful tone, "and I'm Billy the Kid!"

Luke Lemmon was a balding, stocky man of sixty. He wore a handlebar mustache. As Dan approached the general store, Lemmon was briskly applying a broom to the boardwalk. Clouds of dust sifted upward. He eyed Dan carefully as he dismounted and wrapped the reins around the hitching rail.

"'Mornin'," Colt said with a broad smile. "You Mister Lemmon?"

"Was the last time I looked in the mirror," Lemmon said, returning the smile.

"Understand you're in charge of things until the town hires a new marshal."

"You wantin' the job?" asked the stocky man, looking Dan up and down.

"Nope," replied the tall man. "Just need some information."

"I'll try."

"An old feller down the street told me a gang of robbers hit both your banks a few days ago."

"Sure did," replied Lemmon, leaning on the broom. "Killed the marshal and two other men."

"A posse go after 'em?"

"Yeah. Didn't catch 'em, though."

"Which way'd they go?"

"Headed south outta town, then took to the river. For that very reason, we think they swung back north. But we couldn't find where they left the river."

"There were four of 'em?"

"Yep. Masqueradin' as cavalry troopers. Must've stolen the horses and uniforms."

"Nope. Not in that sense," said Dan. "They're deserters."

Lemmon swore. "You a lawman? You after 'em?"

"I'm after 'em," Dan nodded. "But I'm not a lawman."

"How come you're after 'em, then?"

"I was . . . *hired* by Colonel Allen at Fort Ryan to trail 'em and bring 'em in."

"Oh, you're Pinkerton."

"Nope."

"How come the army would have you to go after 'em?"

"It's a long story, Mister Lemmon. But that's what I'm doin'."

Abruptly, Dan's attention was drawn to the Wells

Morgan Hill

Fargo stagecoach as it pulled in from the south end of town, raising a cloud of dust. It was slowing down as it passed Lemmon's General Store. Moving up the street to the Wells Fargo office, it rolled to a stop.

"Nice talkin' to you, Mister Lemmon," said Dan politely.

"Hope you catch them dirty skunks," said Lemmon.

"Where's the gun shop?" asked Colt. "I need some cartridges."

"Right next door to the Fargo office," replied the stocky man, pointing with his nose. "On the other side."

Leading the gelding up the street, Dan said, "Thanks."

People were milling about the stagecoach as Dan walked by and tied the black to the rail in front of the gun shop. A young lady, blond and pretty, was about to enter the stagecoach when her line of sight happened on Dan Colt's face. Her eyes widened, sparked with recognition.

When Colt disappeared into the gun shop, she wheeled and ran into the Fargo office. Excitedly, she said to Sid King, the agent, "I just saw him! He went into the gun shop! I just saw him!"

"Wait a minute, Miss Wells," said King. "Calm down, now. You saw *who*?"

"The man who held up the stage and took my diamond ring!"

King's jaw slacked. "You mean the road agent who shot Herb Freeman and took the thirty-five hundred dollars?"

"Yes!" gasped Marla Wells.

The owner of the gun shop lifted four boxes of .45 cartridges from the shelf and laid them on the counter. Looking into Dan Colt's sky-blue eyes, he said, "That'll be four dollars even, mister."

The tall man laid the money down as the gunsmith wrapped the boxes in brown paper and wound the package carefully with string. Colt thanked the man, ran his finger under the taut string, and walked out the door. As he stepped off the boardwalk and raised the flap of one saddlebag, Dan thought it was strange that all the people had vanished. There was an alien silence that permeated the air, broken only by the blowing of one of the coach horses.

Carefully, he dropped the package in the saddlebag and buckled the strap. Dan's ineffable sixth sense told him that something was awry.

Suddenly two men leaped from behind the coach, leveling shotguns on him. "Reach for the sky!" one of them barked, as two more charged from the doorway of the Fargo office lining rifles on his chest.

Slowly the tall man backed away from the black, lifting his hands skyward.

"Just don't you twitch a finger, blondie," rasped Sid King, holding the shotgun stiffly against his shoulder.

"What's this all about?" asked Dan, fully knowing that once again he was being mistaken for his infamous twin.

Ignoring Dan's question, King looked toward the office door. "You can come on out now, Miss Wells," he said, lifting his voice. Quickly, he turned to the other man holding a shotgun. "Get his guns, Percy."

Morgan Hill

Dan felt his holsters lighten as Percy Smythe relieved him of the twin Colts. Marla Wells emerged from the Fargo office, her face a livid mask of scorn. "That's him!" she breathed angrily. "Changed clothes and got another horse, but *that's him!*"

A crowd of onlookers was gathering. Dan shifted his eyes back and forth. Looking at Sid King, he said, "This is a big mistake, mister. I'm not who you think I am."

Swiftly, Marla Wells stepped off the board sidewalk, skirts rustling, and approached Colt stiff-leggedly. Her eyes were virtual coals of fire. "I want my diamond ring back!" she snapped. Simultaneously, her open right palm met Dan's cheek with a loud pop.

Dan blinked, but held his hands aloft. "Ma'am," he said defensively, "I don't have your diamond ring. This is a case of mistaken identity. I—"

Marla's palm struck him again. Dan felt the heat of the blow on his cheek. "Don't give me that kind of hocus-pocus," she hissed, baring her teeth. "You took the only thing—" The girl's face suddenly twisted sorrowfully and she burst into tears.

A woman of forty-five or fifty detached herself from the crowd, embracing Marla, whose hands now covered her face. "Come, dear," said the woman tenderly. "They'll hold the stage until you can calm down."

Marla stiffened, pulled her hands from her face, and glared at Dan Colt. "I'm not leaving!" she screamed. "I'm not leaving until he's locked up in jail and I have my ring back!"

Forcefully, the woman guided Marla Wells into the Wells Fargo office and closed the door.

"All right, tall timber," said King, motioning southward with the muzzle of the twelve-gauge, "jail's that way."

"I tell you, mister, I don't have the lady's ring. I don't know what this is all about, but—"

"You're tellin' us you didn't hold up the stage 'tween here and Albuquerque last week?"

"That's what I'm tellin' you," said Dan evenly. "I was way south of here last week. I can prove it. If you'll take me to Fort Ryan, it can be easily settled. The commanding officer there can verify that I was with him."

"Are you sayin' Miss Wells is lyin'?" asked one of the men holding a rifle.

From the corner of his eye, Dan saw Luke Lemmon coming up the street in a half-run. "No, she isn't lyin'," said Colt, "She is mistaken. If you'll let me talk with Mister Lemmon, I'll explain it to him."

The heavyset chairman of the town council arrived, mopping his bald head and gasping for breath. Eyeing the situation, he said, "What's going on here?"

"This big fella was identified by Marshal Travers's lady as the dude that held up the stage last week and shot Herb Freeman," said Sid King.

Lemmon squinted, tilted his head sideways, and spoke to Colt. "What you got to say about that?"

"He said she was lyin'," put in Percy Smythe before Dan could reply.

Dan eyed Smythe coldly. "I didn't say she was lyin'. I said she was mistaken." Looking at Sid King, Dan said, "Do I understand that Miss Wells was on the

159

stage last week when it was held up and she was engaged to your marshal?"

"You got it," snapped King.

"So it was her engagement ring the robber took?"

"You got it," repeated the Wells Fargo agent.

Dan shook his head. "No wonder she's upset. With Travers dead, the ring means more to her than ever."

"So why don't you give it back?" King said angrily.

"Because I don't have it," snapped Colt, fixing King with a stone-faced regard. "I'm not the man who held up the stage."

"There's nothing wrong with Marla's eyes," said a man in the crowd.

"There's nothin' wrong with *any* part of her," said another. The crowd laughed.

"There's one way to settle this," offered Luke Lemmon. "Doc Farney's got Herb Freeman over at the hotel. Let's have Herb take a look at him."

"Good idea," said Percy Smythe. "If two of 'em agree, we'll know we have the right *hombre*."

The crowd voiced agreement.

"Okay," said Sid King. Turning to one of the men who held a rifle, he said, "Art, you'd best go ahead and move out with the stage. You'll be late getting to Albuquerque."

Art Cadwell looked at Percy Smythe, his shotgunner, and said, "Whaddya think, Percy?"

"I'd like to stay long enough to know what Herb says," replied Smythe. "It wasn't our stage that was robbed, but I'd like to be able to tell Willie we caught the skunk who shot his gunner."

"Yeah, me too," agreed Cadwell. Tossing his glance

to Sid King, he said, "We'll wait till Herb gets a gander at his puss."

"Hotel's just up the street on the other side," King said to Dan Colt. "Head out."

Turning slowly, Dan walked with reluctance toward the town's only hotel.

Lining the twelve-gauge on Dan's broad back, King spoke to Luke Lemmon. "Luke, you come along."

Lemmon fell in step with King. As they neared the hotel, King spoke to Colt. "You can drop your hands, now. Just don't pull anything funny. You do and I'll bore a hole in you big enough to drive Cadwell's stage through."

Dan lowered his aching arms, massaging the shoulders and biceps. "If you'll just let me explain some things to you . . . and ride to Ryan with me, this'll all clear up," said Colt over his shoulder.

"Let's see what Herb has to say, mister. Then we'll talk." King's voice was cold.

As the trio crossed the lobby with Dan in the lead, the wide-eyed clerk stood behind the desk and stared at the shotgun.

"We want to see Freeman," King told him. "What room's he in?"

"Number three, Mister King," the elderly clerk answered nervously. "He's sitting up, but is still pretty weak. Door's not locked. Just walk in."

As they reached the second floor, King said, "You open the door, big man. We'll be right behind you."

Dan turned the knob and gave it a push. The door squeaked open. Herb Freeman was sitting in an overstuffed chair, facing the door. He had on his trousers and socks. Long underwear was visible from the waist up. His arm was in a sling.

Freeman's gaze lined on Dan's angular face, registered shock, then moved to the other two men. Slowly the shocked look vanished and was replaced with a wide grin. The shotgunner swore. "You got 'im, Sid! How'd you do it?"

CHAPTER FOURTEEN

United States Marshal Logan Tanner swung his big frame stiffly from the saddle and examined the dark brown spots on the boulders. "Blood," he said audibly.

Narrowing his eyes against the sun's reflection off the desert, he studied the numerous patches of blood in the sand and took note of the myriad hoof marks. At first he was convinced that a fierce battle between whites and Comanches had taken place here on the river bank. Closer examination revealed that every horse was shod. There was not a feather anywhere nor an arrow in sight.

The waters of the Rio Grande gurgled pleasingly at the base of the boulders as Tanner and his horse drank from the river. The thick-bodied lawman filled his canteen, studying the bloody scene once again. By the relatively sharp imprints of the hoof marks, he knew the battle had been fought not more than a few days before.

As Tanner lowered himself into the saddle, the big chestnut gelding nickered. Quickly, the big man slid the Winchester from the saddle boot. Squinting, he ran a panorama of the land, expecting to see a band of Comanches closing in. Nothing. The only movement was the shimmering waves of heat on the southern horizon.

The horse nickered again, bobbing his head and looking westward over the river. Tanner could see absolutely no movement on the sun-bleached desert. The gelding nickered repeatedly, staring toward the west.

Suddenly, the marshal saw it. A black dot. The chestnut nickered again. Pulling his hat lower to shade his eyes from the midday sun, Tanner focused on the dark object. It was slowly growing in size. Dismounting again, he stood on the river bank and watched. Within fifteen or twenty minutes, the dark form evolved into the shape of a horse. A riderless horse. Another few minutes revealed the body of a man being dragged by the bay horse. The man's foot was caught in the stirrup.

Running his gaze in a circle again, Tanner satisfied himself there were no Indians about and slid the rifle back in the boot. The chestnut nickered again, this time being answered by the approaching bay. The battered corpse revealed what was left of cavalry blue clothing and as the horse drew up on the opposite bank, Tanner saw the U.S. brand on its hip.

The bay eased down the bank and began drinking lustily. The marshal mounted and rode the chestnut across the river. The bay lifted its head, eyes wide. Water dripped from its mouth.

"Easy, boy," said Tanner as he drew near. The putrid odor of rotting flesh met his nostrils. The poor animal had dragged its dead rider all over the desert and now had returned for water—and to the place of battle.

Climbing the west bank, Logan Tanner held his nose and knelt beside the corpse. Only a portion of the skull remained. The shirt was in shreds. Barely recognizable was a bullet hole centered in the trooper's chest. There wasn't enough shirt left to reveal his rank.

Speaking gently to the horse, the marshal worked the twisted ankle from the stirrup. The leg flopped limply to the ground. Taking a deep breath, Tanner knelt again and rifled the trouser pockets. He found a folded leather case, stood up, and walked away from the sickening stench. Papers in the leather case identified the dead man as Corporal Lonnie M. Ward, C Company out of Fort Ryan.

The path left by Dan Colt, whom Tanner believed was Dave Sundeen, was leading straight up the east side of the Rio Grande. The marshal decided he would bury Ward in the sand of the river bank. Having no shovel, it was the only sensible thing to do. He could dig in the sand with his bare hands. He would take the bay to the fort. A stop there would be necessary anyhow. He would have to see if his man had been there.

Night found the lone lawman stretched out on the bank of the Rio Grande, head on saddle, gazing into the heavens. The horses stood idly by, glad for each other's company. Tanner's eye caught a falling star, followed by a red streamer. Within a minute, another star trailed the first one. The big man thought of himself, trailing the tall, blond outlaw.

Deep within Logan Tanner's soul was a driving force, pushing him relentlessly onward. The unseen impetus was indeed a mystery to the man himself. Many outlaws had crossed Tanner's path. Some had escaped prison, even as Sundeen. Why did he want to capture the man so badly? Was it the scar from the bullet Sundeen had put in him in Holbrook? Was it the man's idiotic fairy tale about a long-lost twin brother? Was it Sundeen's foolish arrogance in claiming to be the famous dead gunhawk, Dan Colt? Or, was it just the outlaw's clandestine elusiveness?

Whatever it was, U.S. Marshal Logan Tanner would not give up. Nothing would deter him. The handsome outlaw who looked like he was born with twin Colts on his hips would be his prisoner once again.

Herb Freeman positively identified Dan Colt as the man who held up the Fargo stage and shot him in the arm. Art Cadwell and Percy Smythe left for Albuquerque with three passengers. Marla Wells was not among them. She remained in Socorro, determined to reclaim her engagement ring.

Luke Lemmon and Sid King ushered Colt into the hot, stuffy jail and locked him in a cell.

"All I ask," said Dan pleadingly, "is that you ride with me to Ryan and let Corporal Allen confirm where I was last week."

"That's not my job," said Lemmon. "It's not Sid's job either."

"I'll wire Raton," put in King. "They'll send a federal man down here. We'll turn you over to him."

Dan instantly thought of Logan Tanner. The big marshal would no doubt reach Socorro before a man could make it from the office at Raton. Either way, Dan was as good as back in Yuma. He had to escape before *any* lawman rode into this town.

"I'll bring you some water," said Lemmon. "You'll get supper at sundown."

Dan opened his mouth to tell them of his twin ... then paused.

"Yeah?" said Lemmon, looking at Dan quizzically.

"Nothin'," replied the tall man dejectedly. They wouldn't believe him. It would only sound like a desperate man's wild story.

The two men left. Dan sat down on the bunk.

An hour passed. Colt heard the outer office door open. Two voices were audible, one masculine, the other feminine.

"You wait here till I take him his water," said Luke Lemmon. "When I've got the door locked again, you can talk to him all you want."

Lemmon appeared in the narrow corridor outside the cells, a wooden bucket in one hand, a Navy Colt .44 in the other. He set the bucket down, slipped the key ring from his belt, and unlocked the door. Toeing the bucket close to the bars beside the door, he backed up to the wall. Lining the muzzle on Colt, he said, "Push the door open and pull the bucket in. Then shut the door and sit back on the bunk."

Dan followed Lemmon's orders. Lowering his muscular frame onto the bunk, he said, "None of you gents have asked my name."

"No need," said Lemmon dryly. "You've already said you ain't the robber. You wouldn't tell us your real name anyway."

Dan shook his head.

"There's a lady out here in the office wants to see you," said Lemmon, locking the door.

"A lady?"

"Miss Wells. She wants to talk to you."

"Okay," said Dan resignedly. "Bring her in."

Lemmon disappeared, then reappeared carrying a chair. Marla Wells followed and stood beside the chair. She wore a full-skirted taffeta dress and a wide-brimmed hat. In her hand was a large purse, which matched her dress. Her large deep-blue eyes still exposed a glint of fire.

"I have to get back to the store, Miss Wells," said Lemmon. "Just stay out of arm's reach and you'll be safe."

Dan threw him a sour look, stood up, and approached the door.

"Oh, by the way," said the merchant to Colt, "the telegraph lines are down. We can't get a message through to Raton. Next stage will have to carry it. Guess you'll be with us a little longer." Looking at the girl, he said, "Just close the outer door when you leave, ma'am."

Marla smiled and nodded.

Lemmon's footsteps faded away and within a few seconds the outer door snapped shut. Still standing, Marla Wells fixed her hot gaze on Dan's face. Pulling her lips tight, she said, "I want my ring, mister."

BANDITS IN BLUE

Dan pressed his forehead to the bars. "Ma'am, I told you before. I don't have it. This whole thing is a case of mistaken ident—"

Marla dipped her hand in the purse and produced a .25 caliber Derringer. She lined the vertically forged barrels between the tall man's eyes. "I know how to use this and I *will*, unless you produce my ring."

"Miss Wells . . . ma'am . . . it was my twin brother who took your ring," said Dan quickly. "I'm trailing him. Trying to capture him. That is . . . I *was*, until you put up the fuss out there in the street. Not that I blame you. My brother and I are identical."

"Some story," iced Marla, unbelief riding her flinty eyes.

"It's the truth, ma'am," said Dan softly. "I can do no more than tell you the truth."

Holding the gun steadily, the blond-headed girl said, "A man will lie through his teeth to save his skin."

"I won't argue with that, ma'am. But does that make me a liar?"

"Why should I believe you?" she hissed.

"You have no reason to believe me, Miss Wells," Dan answered calmly, "but how will you feel when you kill me and then find out you shot an innocent man?"

Marla's face muscles relaxed. The words of the astute man had their effect. Seeing this, Dan followed with more. "Either I'm lying or I'm telling the truth, ma'am. Right?"

The girl had not relaxed her gun hand. The deadly barrels glared at Dan's face. "Yes," she answered.

"Then the odds are fifty-fifty that I'm the wrong man. Will you kill me on those odds?"

Marla Wells's eyes grew misty. Her beautiful face lost its hardness. Slowly she lowered the Derringer until the muzzles pointed at the rough wooden floor. Her lower lip quivered. Looking Dan square in the eye, she said tearfully, "Ben Travers is all I had in the world, Mister—"

"Colt, ma'am. Dan Colt."

"Those robbers killed him, Mister Colt. They took all I had in this world." Tears were now spilling down her cheeks. "Ben gave me that engagement ring. I was coming here to marry him. Can you understand what the ring means?"

"Certainly, ma'am. I understand. I—"

"How could you?" she blurted. "You couldn't understand. You couldn't unless you had lost someone . . . had them shot down like Ben was. You would have to—"

"I did, Miss Wells," butted in Dan Colt.

"Wha—?"

"I *did*, ma'am. Could I tell you about it?"

Marla sank into the chair. She dropped the Derringer into her purse. Pulling a hankie from the same purse, she dabbed at her eyes and said, "Yes, Mister Colt. I would like to hear about it. Maybe it would relieve some of this pain inside me to talk to someone who knows how I feel."

Dan pulled up a small stool from next to the bunk and sat down. Looking at her sitting in the chair, tears flowing, his heart went out to the girl. "It's hot in here, ma'am. Would you like some of my water?"

"Yes," she answered, swallowing hard. "I'd appreciate it."

Dan stood up, dipped a tin cup into the wooden bucket, and carried it to the bars. "I'll set the cup out there on the floor, ma'am. Then I'll back up to the far wall so you can pick it up."

Marla Wells's countenance was totally changed. Her lip still quivered slightly as she spoke. "I'm not afraid of you, Mister Colt. Don't ask me why, but somehow I know you wouldn't harm me." Straightening in the chair, she stood up and took the cup from the tall, handsome man. Lifting it to her mouth, she drained the cup. Handing it back, she managed a smile. "Thank you."

Dan dipped himself a cupful, downed it, and moved back to the stool. Marla returned to the chair.

Dan Colt began his story with the day he met Mary on a busy Wichita street. He told Marla of their wedding and subsequent move to the Wyoming ranch. Carefully, he described the great love that he had for the lovely Mary.

Marla wept again as Dan told of Mary's brutal murder. She listened intently as he described how he brought each killer to retribution.

Her voice cracking, Marla said, "I'm sorry, Mister Colt. I guess I've been wallowing in self-pity. It has helped me to talk to you."

"You don't need to be sorry, ma'am. But I'm glad it has helped you."

"Why are you after your twin? You're not a lawman."

"That's another story, ma'am."

"I'd like to hear it."

The tall man began this story at Holbrook, Arizona, where Logan Tanner arrested him as Dave Sundeen. He told of the five horrible months in Yuma Prison and of the escape. He continued, bringing her up to the present moment.

"It's been a living nightmare, hasn't it?" she said tenderly.

"Yes'm," agreed Dan. "Now it's gonna get worse. Tanner's breathing down my neck. If he gets tired of waiting at Fort Ryan and finds me, not having seen the affidavit, it's back to Yuma."

"That's not going to happen," Marla said, standing up.

"What?" said Dan, eyeing her doubtfully.

"I'm getting you out of here."

Dan stood up, wide-eyed.

"If I get you out of here, you can bring Ben's killers to justice . . . and maybe if you find Dave, you can get my ring back."

"But—"

"No buts about it." With that, she turned and went into the outer office.

"But, ma'am. They'll have the law after you." Dan's face was pressed to the bars.

Frustration was on Marla's face as she returned. "Lemmon must have kept the keys on his belt. I can't find them." Digging into the purse, she produced the Derringer. Pushing it through the bars, she said, "Here. Put this on him when he brings your supper."

"But, ma'am, they'll know you gave it to me. You could go to prison."

"It would be worth it to know you caught Ben's killers."

"There has to be a way to keep you out of this," said Dan. "No sense in you having to—"

Dan's words were cut off with the sound of the outer door opening. Quickly, he reached through the bars and wrapped a muscular arm gently around her neck. Carefully, he pressed her back to the bars and pointed the Derringer at her head. She did not resist. She knew what Dan was doing.

Luke Lemmon came through the door carrying a tray of food. His mouth flew open, eyes bulging.

"Unlock the door, Lemmon," Dan barked. "I'll kill 'er!"

"Get ahold of yourself, son," the older man said nervously.

"Hurry up," snapped Dan.

Riveting his eyes on the tall man, Luke Lemmon placed the tray on the floor. Slipping the key off his belt, he unlocked the door. Marla played her part, looking frightened.

When the door swung open, Dan released the girl and put the muzzle on the chairman of Socorro's town council. "Get in the cell," Dan commanded, stepping into the corridor.

"You, too, ma'am."

"How did this happen?" Lemmon asked Marla.

"She came here to kill me," put in Dan. "Got too close. I grabbed her." Closing the door, he turned the key. "Now Mister Lemmon, I hate doing this. But you left me no choice. A simple ride to Fort Ryan would have cleared me. When it's all over, I'll come back and buy you a steak dinner."

"I sure hope so, son," said Lemmon.

"Good-bye, Miss Wells," Dan said pleasantly. "If I ever recover your ring, where will I find you?"

"Right here, Mister Colt. Right here." Marla's eyes were telling Dan to come back, even without the ring. She wanted to know when the killers were caught. "I'm staying in Socorro."

"Where are my guns, Mister Lemmon?"

"In the cabinet behind the desk," Lemmon said with disdain.

"The keys will be on the desk," said Dan. Looking back to Marla, he said, "I'll do my best, ma'am."

"I know you will," responded Marla. "Mister Colt . . ."

"Yes, ma'am."

"I'm sorry I put the gun on you."

"It's all right, ma'am. I understand."

"Good-bye," she said.

"*Adiós*," said the tall man . . . and was gone.

CHAPTER FIFTEEN

Dave Sundeen watched the young deputy angle across the dusty Albuquerque street and enter the sheriff's office. He led the big buckskin up the block from the place where he was positioned. It was eight o'clock.

Wrapping the reins around the hitching rail, the tall man ducked underneath and crossed the boardwalk. Glancing both ways before entering the office, Dave noted that the street was empty.

Deputy Leon Hatch was not in the office as Dave entered. Voices were coming from the rear area. Sundeen waited. Presently, Hatch appeared, along with a scuzzy-looking man whose eyes were swollen and bloodshot.

The deputy gave the towering Sundeen a pleasant look and moved behind the desk. From a drawer, he produced a gun and holster. Extending it to the foul-smelling man, he said, "Here's your gun, Norm. Now, you'd best get out of town before those men you threatened show up."

"I didn't mean none of them things I said," said Norm defensively. "I just had a leetle too much to drink."

"I'm not sure you'll convince the Diamond-T boys of that. You just move on, okay?"

Norm nodded, buckled on the gun, and staggered out the door. The deputy put his eyes on Dave Sundeen. "What can I do for you, mister?"

Feigning ignorance, Dave said, "Sheriff around?"

"No, sir," replied Hatch. "He's up in Santa Fe. Won't be back for two-three more days."

Sundeen felt a wave of relief wash over him.

"My name's Leon Hatch," said the young deputy. "Can I be of service?"

Swinging his head for a casual look out the windows, Dave checked the street. All clear. As he turned back his right-hand Colt jumped into his hand. Hatch's eyes widened.

"I have to detain you for a little while today," said Dave, lips drawn tight. "Drop your gun belt."

Releasing the buckle, Hatch said, "What's this all about?"

"You'll know a little later," said Sundeen. "Now, deputy, I'm gonna lock you in one of your cells. I don't want to hurt you. You can go peaceably, or with a knot on your head. Choice is yours."

"You've got the gun, mister," said Hatch morosely. "I never did like pain. I'll go peaceably." He turned and walked to the cell area.

In less than five minutes, Dave had the deputy locked in a cell, bound, and gagged. He had entered the office area and was searching for the sign that was used to signify the office was closed. He spied it lying on a shelf when the door came open. A pretty young girl whom Dave judged to be about nineteen entered carrying a pan of hot muffins.

The girl looked at Dave and smiled. A feeling of frustration pricked at his stomach. He disliked having to manhandle a female. "Good morning," she said cheerfully. "Is Leon—I mean . . . is Deputy Hatch here?"

"He . . . uh . . . went out back, ma'am," said Dave, hoping she would think Hatch was visiting the privy. To his relief, she did.

"Oh," the girl said, eyes fluttering. "Will you give these to him? He'll know where they came from."

"Sure will, ma'am," replied the tall man. The girl laid the pan on the desk over a newspaper and started out the door. Frustration stabbed Sundeen's midsection again as he heard a male voice greet the girl.

" 'Morning, Mister Willoughby," she said in a friendly tone.

A spindly man of forty entered the office. Smiling at Dave, he said, "Howdy, stranger." His eyes did a double take and he said, "Oh, you're that Dan Colt fella who bored a couple holes in 'Bad Boy' Braden yesterday. Say, Mister Colt, that was *some* shootin'! I've heard a lot—"

"Name's not Colt, sir," said Dave evenly.

"But Mister Byas says he knows you and he says you're Dan Colt."

Dave saw no use in arguing the point. The task at this moment was to get rid of whatzizname Willoughby. Then the thought struck him. Why not let them think he *was* Dan Colt? After the banks were robbed, it might send some heat in Colt's direction, wherever he was.

"I guess Mister Byas has a good eye, huh?" said Dave, winking.

"See there . . . I thought so," said Willoughby, winking back and sending a bony elbow into Sundeen's ribs. "Deputy around?"

"He's . . . uh . . . out back," said Dave with a toss of his head.

"Oh," said Willoughby, smiling furtively, looking that direction. "Think he'll be long?"

"Might be tied up quite awhile," responded Dave.

"Well, I can see him later. Tell him I dropped by. Name's Willoughby. Fred Willoughby."

"Sure will, Fred," smiled Sundeen.

Willoughby started through the door. Dave's relief was checked as the man stopped, turned around, and said, "That sure was some shootin', Mister Colt. Some shootin'!"

Dave nodded, smiling, and Willoughby was gone. Quickly, the tall man palmed the sign, stuck it in the window, and stepped out on the boardwalk. Mounting hastily, he looked back at the sign, which read:

SHERIFF OUT
WILL RETURN LATER

Working fast, Dave deposited the buckskin at the Rio Grande Corral and walked to the south edge of town. Ken Deere was waiting with the army bay. Under cover of the cottonwoods, Sundeen donned the blue uniform, strapped on the pistol and saber, and placed the hat, bearing the crossed sabers, on his head.

Fidgeting with the high-riding holster, Dave said, "I sure feel unbalanced with this thing practically up to my armpit. Hope I don't meet up with Wyatt Earp, Bat Masterson, or *Dan Colt*." Dave tossed a look at Alex Hopper as he said it.

Hopper smiled. "Especially Colt."

Sundeen stuffed his gear in the saddlebags. "Let's get going, boys," he said. "It'll be just before ten o'clock when we ride up to the first bank."

Admiring eyes watched the five "cavalrymen" rein in at the hitching rail of the Albuquerque Bank and Trust. It was a few minutes before opening time. Dave was relieved to see that there were no customers waiting out front. He slipped the ready-made sign from the saddlebag.

Joe Caraway made his way to the door and rapped on the window. After a few seconds, he rapped again. Presently, a wrinkled face adorned with silver hair and moustache appeared in the window. "We don't open until ten," the man said loudly.

"This is important," said Caraway, with impatience.

The man then recognized the uniforms and smiled. The lock rattled and the door came open. "What is it, sergeant?"

Quickly, Caraway barged in, drawing his gun. Behind him came Dave Sundeen, followed by Ken Deere and Frank Stevens. Alex Hopper maintained his position just outside the door. The operation was fast and smooth. The four men emerged carrying money bags. Sundeen stuck the sign in the door window.

"Everything all right?" asked Hopper.

"Got 'em all tied up," replied Caraway.

Two businessmen were approaching the bank as the "troopers" were mounting up. They eyed the money bags and looked quizzically at the five men in blue. Joe Caraway spoke up from the back of his horse. "Bank'll be closed for a little while, gentlemen. Got word there's some robbers in the area. We're movin' the money out for safekeeping."

Both men smiled broadly. "Good for you, sergeant," said one.

Dropping the money in their saddlebags, the five men trotted the horses up the street and pulled in at the Bank of New Mexico. Dave Sundeen eyed the sign in the door window at the sheriff's office across the street. He was relieved that it was undisturbed. The street was now heavy with traffic and busy with people. Some stopped and watched the uniformed men dismount and enter the bank.

"What's goin' on?" one man asked Alex Hopper, who halted at the door.

"Little precautionary protection," replied Hopper. "There's a gang of bank robbers in the area. We're movin' the money out. Gonna fool 'em."

The man laughed. "They'll be surprised, huh?"

"Yeah," Alex chuckled nervously.

Suddenly, from inside, a shot rang out. Immediately the door burst open. Stevens and Deere came out on the run, bearing money bags. "Get on your horse!" Deere hollered at Hopper.

The small crowd stood stunned, not believing what

BANDITS IN BLUE

they were seeing. Shortly, Caraway and Sundeen emerged. Dave was angry.

"I thought he was reachin' for a gun," the tall, slender Caraway said, defensively.

As they mounted, a man in the crowd was going for his gun. Joe eyed him, raised his already smoking gun, and fired. Women screamed as the mortally wounded man fell to the dust.

Galloping northward, Hopper shouted, "We gonna pass the third bank?"

"No!" answered Dave Sundeen. "We'll never have another chance like this. We'll have to make it fast, but we might as well get what we can!"

Drawing rein in a cloud of dust, the five men leaped from their saddles. Sundeen spoke with acid in his voice. "Joe, you wait out here. Ken will go inside with me. There'll be some men chargin' up the street shortly. Shoot over their heads and hold 'em back."

"Now look," bit back Caraway, "I'm goin' inside!"

"You do as I tell you!" snapped Sundeen. Without hesitation, he spun on his heels. Ken Deere followed hastily. As the two passed through the door, they could hear Joe Caraway cursing savagely.

"You get the tellers," Dave said to Ken. "I'll hit the safe."

Leaving Deere to handle the tellers and two female customers who stood at the windows, Dave walked to the desk where Henry Byas sat poring over some important-looking papers. He lifted his eyes as Dave approached the desk. His line of sight fell on the uniform, then Dave's face . . . then the muzzle of the gun. "What is it, lieut—?". The obese bank president blinked and squinted at the tall man who stood over him. "Colt, what the—?"

"I want the money from the vault, Mister Byas. I want it right now."

Flustered and shocked, Byas worked his way out of the chair. As Dave followed him to the vault, gunfire erupted in the street.

"You've always been one of my heroes, Colt," said Byas, filling a canvas bag with currency. "I always thought you were on the side of the law."

"Times are tough," said Dave sharply.

Another minute brought Deere and Sundeen through the door. Caraway, Stevens, and Hopper were firing at men down the street. Dave noticed that two lifeless forms lay a block away in the dust.

"I told you to shoot over their heads!" roared Sundeen, swinging into the saddle. His eyes were on Joe Caraway. The latter did not answer. He snapped another shot down the street and the five bandits galloped northward out of town.

They paused long enough to cut the telegraph line in two places, then rode hard for over an hour, angling eastward into the Sandias. Once in the cover of the mountains, they picked their way among the rocks and crevices. By early afternoon, they found a spot among the tall trees amid a cluster of large rocks.

"Looks pretty good here," said Sundeen. "Okay with you, boys?"

Each man nodded and voiced agreement except Joe Caraway. His face was stiff and sullen. It did not go unnoticed by Dave Sundeen.

One by one, the men began actively setting up

camp. Except Joe Caraway. He sat brooding on a large rock. Sundeen strode to where Caraway sat. Standing over him, he said, "I understand about the men in the street, Joe, maybe that had to be. But there was no need in killing that banker."

Caraway looked up, fixing his hot gaze on Sundeen's face. "I told you. I thought he was goin' for a gun."

"He was six feet from his desk," Dave said, his voice raw. "Where was he going to get a gun? He wasn't wearin' a coat. There couldn't possibly have been a gun concealed in that tight-fitting vest."

"I don't need you ridin' my back every time I pull a trigger," said Caraway. He spoke softly, but there was something in his voice warning that he would not be pushed. Dave thought of him as a bottle of nitroglycerin riding a buckboard on a bumpy road. If he was jostled just right, he could be extremely dangerous.

"We agreed," said Dave. "No unnecessary killing."

"Okay, Dave," said Joe, shrugging his shoulders. "I'm sorry. I got a little jumpy. It won't happen again."

"Good," smiled Sundeen, cuffing the sergeant lightly on the chin. "Camp's about set up. Let's count the loot."

Darkness was enshrouding the rugged Sandias as the five men in blue sat in a circle around a smokeless fire. Each man was elated. The total take was over seventy-six thousand dollars, giving each one over fifteen thousand.

"What's next?" asked Alex Hopper, excitement in his eyes.

"We'll catch a stagecoach or two on the way to Santa Fe, then clean out both banks there," said Joe Caraway. "We'll cut some more telegraph lines and move into Colorado."

Dave Sundeen stood up and shoved dirt on the fire with his boots. "Better keep it dark," he said. "Make it harder for a posse to locate us."

"You really think they'd follow us this far into the mountains?" asked Ken Deere.

"Would *you*, for seventy-six thousand dollars?" parried Sundeen.

"Guess so," replied Deere.

The five men in blue settled down for the night. The wind played a mournful tune in the treetops.

It was shortly before dawn when Dave Sundeen came instantly wide awake. His sixth sense was shooting prickly needles up and down his spine. The other four men were sound asleep. Cautiously, the tall outlaw rolled to his knees. Stuffing saddlebags under his blanket as he had done not so long ago, he placed his flat-crowned hat where his face would be. Quietly, he crept among the trees, the twin Colts in his hands. Finding a crevice among some large boulders, he sat down where he had a full view of the camp.

Off to the left, he thought he heard movement among the trees. Peering through the dissipating darkness, he could see nothing.

Dawn's gray was turning pink when Dave saw Joe Caraway sit up, stretch, and look around at the other prostrate forms. Caraway stood up, scratching his upper body and running his fingers through his straw-colored hair. He gathered sticks and pine needles. Lighting a match, he set the small heap on fire.

Suddenly, seven men bearing rifles moved into the camp in a perfect circle. "Grab the sky!" bellowed one man.

Shocked, Joe Caraway shoved his empty hands upward. The men on the ground began to stir. "All right, let's have the rest of you on your feet!" rasped another posse member.

Dave Sundeen knew he had only a brief moment to get in position before they discovered the saddlebags under his blanket. Lining up with a big pine tree, he ran in a straight line and squared his back against the rough bark. He was now within ten yards of the campsite. Edging around the tree, Dave saw that all four of his cohorts were on their feet, hands raised.

One of the posse members broke into a string of curse words as the limp blanket left the toe of his boot. As the other six began to scan the perimeter of the circle, Dave lunged on the scene. Both .45's had their hammers dogged back.

"Drop 'em!" roared Sundeen.

The man who had kicked away Dave's blanket swung his gun around. Sundeen's left-hand Colt belched fire. The bullet tore into the man's shoulder, slamming him to the ground. One of the other posse men started to bring his rifle to bear, then checked himself as Dave eyed him savagely. "Drop it!" Sundeen bellowed.

Simultaneously, all six men dropped their rifles.

"Now the gun belts," Dave snapped. "Pick 'em up, boys."

As the men in blue gathered up the firearms, Dave donned his hat and lined the posse in a sitting position on the ground. The wounded man was conscious, lying flat, cursing his pain.

"Hold your guns on 'em, boys," said Dave, "while I check his wound." Kneeling beside the man, he tore open his shirt. Studying it for a moment, he said, "Bullet's still in there."

The wounded man said, "You don't care who you shoot, do you, Colt? One day it's 'Bad Boy' Braden, the next it's a man trying to do a job for his town."

"I wouldn't have shot you if you'd done what I told you," rasped Sundeen.

The man grimaced, sucking air.

"You can't let him die," said one of the others. "You've got to get him to a doctor."

"We'll do the best we can," said Dave. "Isn't there a Fargo stage out of Santa Fe this morning?"

"Yeah," answered the same man. "If it's on time, it'll pass the road straight off this mountain about tenthirty."

Ken Deere produced a pocket watch. "We can make it if we head out."

Within fifteen minutes, the blue-clad bandits rode away from the campsite, leaving the Albuquerque posse to walk home. Harold Bender, the wounded man, was limply astride his own horse. Six riderless horses were led by the bandits.

The posse cursed as the horsemen disappeared into the trees.

CHAPTER SIXTEEN

Harold Bender slumped low in the saddle as the horses climbed the last steep slope before they would top out and descend to the desert floor. As the riders reached the crest, Joe Caraway pointed northward. The mountains around Santa Fe stood tall and still against the azure sky.

A cloud of dust was visible against the cactus and sagebrush. "Santa Fe stage," observed Caraway. "We'll have to shake a leg or it'll pass by before we reach the road."

Dave Sundeen threw a backward glance at the wounded man. "Bender can't ride fast. Rest of you fellas stay with him and bring him down slow. I'll take Alex with me and we'll stop the stage. We'll hold it there until you arrive."

"We're gonna clean it out before we let it go on to Albuquerque, aren't we?" asked Frank Stevens.

"You bet we will," butted in Caraway. Turning to

Sundeen, he said, "I'll go ahead and stop the stage. You stay with Bender."

Sundeen's face stiffened. "We'll do it like I said."

Caraway was ready to make an argument of it, but one look at Sundeen's locked expression told him to leave it alone.

Dave rode to the slack form of Harold Bender. Speaking softly, he said, "Bender. You okay?"

The man slowly raised his head, adjusted the makeshift sling Sundeen had tied on him, and nodded painfully.

"I'm riding ahead to stop the stage. We'll put you on it and have you in Albuquerque in short order."

Bender nodded again, looking at the ground.

"Let's go, Alex," said Dave. His gaze fell on Joe Caraway's dark, sullen face.

Sundeen and Hopper galloped down the slope, heading for the road. The stage was weaving along the dusty trail, horses straining into the harness. High on the slope, the descending group watched as the two riders and the coach moved together.

Planting his horse in the middle of the rutted trail, Sundeen began waving his hat. Hopper sat his horse off to the side. Tightening the reins, the driver drew the stagecoach to a halt. Passengers leaned out both sides, observing the two men in cavalry blue. The shotgunner remained relaxed.

As the breeze carried the billowing dust away, the driver said, "What is it, trooper?"

Dave touched the bay's sides with his heels and rode up to the coach. He recognized the driver about three seconds before the driver recognized him. Whipping out the revolver on his side, Dave said, "Keep your hands on the reins, driver." Shifting his gaze to the shotgunner, he said, "Let it slide to the ground."

Holding the reins tightly, Willie Penn said, "Do as he says, Randy. This is the same sleazy rat who shot Herb." As the gunner let the twelve-gauge slip from his fingers, Willie threw a glance at Alex Hopper, who lined his revolver on the four passengers. "Looks like he found another rat in the nest for his partner."

"We've got a wounded man coming down from the mountains," said Sundeen, tossing his head eastward. Penn squinted at the dark figures weaving carefully down the slope. "Need you to take him into Albuquerque."

"Let him rot," snapped Penn. "You and your kind deserve everything you get."

"The wounded man isn't one of us," retaliated Sundeen. "He's part of a posse that was chasin' us. Has a bullet in his shoulder. Name's Harold Bender. You know him?"

Willie Penn's face tightened. "Sure I know him. "Mighty fine feller, too."

"Get the passengers out of the stage, Alex," Dave said, without moving his eyes off the driver.

Hopper dismounted and waved the muzzle of his revolver at the four well-dressed men who occupied the coach. "All right, gentlemen, everybody out."

Nervously, the men exited the dust-covered coach and huddled together. "Now, let's have your wallets, watches, rings, and the like," said Hopper, extending his free hand.

"You'll never get away with this," hissed the eldest of the four. "I'll see that your commanding officer hears of this. You'll stand before a firing squad."

"Why don't you tell him about it right now?" asked Hopper.

"Huh?"

"The lieutenant there is my commanding officer."

"You know what I mean," the man said angrily.

As Hopper collected the wallets, he examined them. Arching his eyebrows, he looked at Sundeen, who still sat on his horse. "Hey, lieutenant. These here are big-shot bankers."

Sundeen eyed them with interest. "Where you gentlemen headed?"

"We don't have to tell you anything!" rasped the banker on the far left. Sundeen's gun roared. The man's face blanched as his hat flipped to the ground, rolled, and flopped in the dust.

"I asked you a question," Dave said evenly, blue smoke sifting from the muzzle of his gun.

"L-Las C-Cruces," answered the hatless man. "W-we're going to est-establish a new bank th-there."

"Carryin' any money?" queried Sundeen.

"No."

"There's about two hundred between 'em in the wallets," Hopper said advisedly, stuffing the money in his shirt pocket.

Sundeen tossed a glance toward the mountains. The slow-moving riders were now on the flat.

"Search the coach," Dave commanded Hopper. "See what you can find. I want to let it go as soon as they get here with Bender."

Fifteen minutes later, Alex Hopper was emptying a cash box bound for the Fargo office in Albuquerque. It contained nearly eleven hundred dollars. There was no other money on the stage.

Joe Caraway and his riders closed in. Quickly, Harold Bender was placed in the coach. The banker whose hat bore a hole volunteered to ride on top of the coach. Bender could have his seat. As he scrambled to his lofty perch and the other three climbed inside, Ken Deere spoke up. "Dave! There's a stagecoach approaching from the south. Comin' out of Albuquerque."

Sundeen narrowed his eyes against the sun's bright glare and focused on the cloud of dust. His brain went to work. If he let the two coaches meet, not only would it detain Bender, but the other coach would be informed as to the present robbery.

Making a snap decision, he said to Willie Penn, "I'm turnin' you loose now. Bender needs medical attention *pronto*. We'll be right behind you. Don't stop for the other stagecoach. Just put your horses into a dead run and don't stop till you hit Albuquerque. Understand?"

"Yessir," said Penn.

"Now, git!" cried Sundeen with a swing of his arm.

With the crack of Penn's whip and his hearty "Hyah!," the six horses lunged into the harness. The slender coach weaved heavily and blended into the lifting dust.

"We'll stop the other coach as soon as they pass each other," shouted Sundeen. "Let's go!"

Leaving Harold Bender's horse behind, the bandits in blue raced southward to the sound of thundering hooves. Riding against the hot wind, they watched intently as the two stagecoaches neared the meeting point. Abruptly, Willie Penn veered his vehicle off the road to the west, giving the oncoming stage right-of-way.

The driver and shotgunner on the northbound stage waved their hats furiously, but Penn paid no heed. Within seconds, his speeding vehicle had rounded a wide bend, topped a gradual rise, and disappeared. Only his dust cloud remained in sight.

Clapping their hats back on their heads, Art Cadwell and Percy Smythe caught sight of the cavalry troopers bracing themselves in the middle of the road. Cadwell cried, "Whoa!" and bore back on the reins.

The bobbing stagecoach rolled to a stop. One of the passengers inside was swearing.

"What's happenin', lieutenant?" Cadwell asked Sundeen.

At the moment Dave spoke, both driver and shotgunner focused on his face and turned to each other.

"Little robbery, gents," said Sundeen. "You with the shotgun, let it drop to the prairie dogs."

Smythe obeyed. The shotgun hit the ground with a clatter. The two Wells Fargo employees looked at each other again.

"You inside the coach," bellowed Joe Caraway, "come out into the sunshine!"

Two women in their late sixties and a man about forty-five climbed out, facing five guns.

"Some way for cavalry troopers to act," snapped the heaviest of the two women. "Oughtta be ashamed of yourselves!"

Ignoring the outburst, Dave said to the man, "Drop your gunbelt, sir." As the man complied, Sundeen scanned the faces of the men in blue. "Alex, you help me keep 'em covered. Rest of you clean out the coach and relieve these nice people of their valuables."

Joe Caraway's face flushed. His jaw clenched hard. "Why do I have to do the dirty work?" Eyes flashing fire at Sundeen, he said, "Why can't I hold a gun on 'em and *you* claw for the money?"

"You know why," said Dave curtly. "Hurry up."

With heated reluctance, Caraway joined the others.

Up on the seat, Art Cadwell whispered to Percy Smythe, "It ain't possible! He's locked up in Socorro!"

"No he ain't!" argued Smythe in the same whisper. "Ain't your brain workin'?"

"Hey, you two!" roared Sundeen. "What's all the whispering about?"

"Uh . . . er . . . uh . . . we was jist discussin' what we heard in Albuquerque," said Cadwell.

"What's that?"

"Uh . . . 'bout them cavalry troopers what held up all three banks yestidday. You must be them."

"You're mighty observant, driver," said Dave.

"You the same *hombres* that hit the banks in Socorro a couple days afore thet?"

"Might be."

"Well, you fellers better cool it if you're headed for Santa Fe!"

Smythe eyed Cadwell blankly.

"Oh?" said Sundeen.

"Yeah," Cadwell said confidently. "Folks in Albuquerque telegraphed the sheriff in Santa Fe. They're ready for you up there!"

"Did, eh?"

"Yep."

"How'd they do that with the wires down?"

"Eh?"

"I said, how did they telegraph Santa Fe with the wires down?"

"Wires ain't down," Percy Smythe put in hurriedly. He was onto Cadwell's game.

"We cut 'em as we rode out of town yesterday," Dave said with a half-smile.

"They got the message off before you cut the wires," lied Caldwell. "It was acknowledged. So they know it got through."

A flash of heat touched Sundeen's stomach. Maybe they *did* get a message through.

"We got about a thousand in a cash box and a few dollars off these folks," said Ken Deere, standing in front of the three passengers. The open cash box lay at his feet.

"No jewelry?" asked Dave.

"Nothin' worth takin'."

"Take it anyway," snapped Joe Caraway, who stood next to the coach.

"Why?" asked the heavier woman. "You going to wear my earrings?"

Caraway's already frayed temper blinded him. Stepping to the woman, he jerked off both her earrings. Her right hand made a perfect arc and slapped his face ferociously. Stunned, the slender man took one step back and punched her hard with his right fist.

As the woman slumped earthward, Sundeen was out of the saddle, charging at Caraway. Putting his hand on Joe's chest, he slammed him against the stagecoach and lifted the woman to her feet.

Caraway righted himself, breathing hard, bolting

BANDITS IN BLUE

Sundeen with a hard glare. Dave eyed him with blurred fury and assisted the woman into the stagecoach. "I'm sorry, ma'am," he said apologetically, "the sergeant has a nasty disposition."

The woman moaned as she eased into the seat. The other two passengers climbed in. Dave closed the door. Alex Hopper still held his gun on the driver and gunner.

"We gonna let 'em go to Santa Fe?" Frank Stevens asked Sundeen. "If the driver's lyin' and they're not expectin' us, they sure *will* be if we let 'em go."

"We'll pick another direction," replied Sundeen. "Can't take the chance now."

Art Cadwell looked down and smiled. His adept stretching of the truth would spare Santa Fe's banks from being robbed.

Joe Caraway spoke up heatedly. "You know he's lyin'. Why not just put a bullet in each head and take off for Santa Fe?"

Dave Sundeen's stern face was marked with dark shadows. "You shut up, Caraway. You haven't got the brains of a sunstroked salamander."

Caraway's face reddened. He answered nothing and made no move.

Looking up at Cadwell, Sundeen said, "Take off, driver."

The vehicle lunged forward with the rattle of traces and was instantly hidden in a dust cloud.

"Let's move back to the mountains and talk things over," said Dave Sundeen. "We'll move north of where that sore-footed posse will come out."

The midafternoon sun found the five bandits seated in a circle, each man counting his part of the loot. Alex Hopper smiled broadly. "This stagecoach robbing makes a nice fill-in between banks. I'm feelin' rich already."

"Not bad for a day's work," agreed Ken Deere. "Isn't there another stage out of Albuquerque in a couple days?"

"Should be," said Frank Stevens. "The one we just hit will be back from Raton day after tomorrow, too."

"Why don't we hit both of them and let things cool off before we try any more banks?" said Deere.

"Might be a good idea," agreed Sundeen. "Those stages pay pretty good."

"Not as good as banks," iced Joe Caraway. "If pretty boy, here, had listened to me, we could have picked up another forty-fifty thousand in Santa Fe."

"What's eatin' you, Joe?" asked Dave. "You were all red-hot for me joining up a few days ago. Now, you act like you regret it."

"I ain't runnin' things like before," said Caraway morosely. "You act like somebody appointed you boss."

"Somebody with brains and common sense has got to run this show," rasped Sundeen. "You're too trigger-happy and hotheaded."

"It was you who shot Bender," Caraway snarled.

"I didn't kill him like you would've."

"Oh, you're a shining saint, huh?"

"Not at all, buster, but I'm not kill-hungry. And another thing," added Dave, "if I ever see you rough up a woman again, I'll tie you in a knot so tight you'll have to spread your toes to eat."

Caraway jumped to his feet, slamming his hat to

the ground. Sundeen stood up to face him. The others slowly came to their feet. The two blond-headed men stood almost the same height. Sundeen was taller by about an inch and outweighed Caraway some twenty pounds.

Heatedly, Caraway said through his teeth, "I'm sick of your pure-dee Sunday School ways . . . and I'm double-sick of taking orders from a Sunday School teacher. I'm boss of this outfit, you savvy?"

Dave scanned the faces of the other men. "Did you boys cast a ballot for Joe as boss?"

Silently, with a little fear, the three men shook their heads. Sundeen's ice-blue eyes swung back to Caraway. "Looks like you're a self-appointed hotshot."

"I'm boss," hissed Joe.

"Not mine, you're not," retaliated Dave.

"If you stay in this outfit, I am. Those lieutenant bars don't impress me."

Looking at Deere, Dave said, "You want to be boss?"

"Nope."

Moving his gaze to Hopper, he said, "You?"

"No."

Lining on Stevens, he said, "You?"

"Huh-uh."

Looking Joe square in the eye, Dave said, "Too many chiefs and too few Indians will mess up the operation."

"I agree," said Caraway evenly.

"Looks like we gotta see who has to take orders from who," said Sundeen.

"Looks like it," snipped Caraway.

"You've been itchin' anyway."

"You're right."

Sundeen's reflex, born of more than his share of fights, moved his head as Caraway's right fist whistled by. Dave drove his fist piston-style into Joe's belly. Air whooshed from his mouth as he doubled over. Sundeen chopped him with a hard left behind the ear. Joe went down, rolled over, and kicked the broad-shouldered man in the groin.

Dave buckled and Caraway kicked him in the face. As Joe rose to his feet, he closed in. Sundeen staggered slightly, taking a right on the jaw. He countered with a hard left that buckled Caraway's knees. It was evident to the three observers that the ex-sergeant would never last trading punches with a mountain of muscle like Dave Sundeen.

Nausea picked at Sundeen from the bruised groin. Breathing deeply, he tried to shake it off. Caraway took advantage of the brief respite, to shake the cobwebs from his head. Dave came in again, like a freight train, fists pumping like steel rods. He clipped the tip of Joe's chin, dodged a right hook, and slammed a savage punch to his jaw. Caraway's knees buckled again, but his fury held him up. He found Dave's left forehead with a popping right, missed with the left.

Sundeen punched him twice in the nose, bringing salty water to Caraway's eyes. Joe blinked, attempting to clear his vision. He didn't see where it came from, but a hissing right cross found his jaw. The world flipped upside down as the ground flew up and hit him hard. The trees seemed to fall into the sky. The towering Sundeen stood over him, sliding in and out of focus.

The bigger man's voice kept fading in and out. Finally, Joe distinguished what Dave was saying, just as the world righted itself and Sundeen's face came clear. "Stay down, Joe! Stay down!"

Caraway summoned all his strength and aimed one more punch at Sundeen's jaw. He never knew whether it landed or not. Bone in his face crunched and the lights went out.

With Caraway flat on the ground, out cold, Dave said, "One of you boys splash some water in his face and bring him around. We've got to make plans for hitting both of those stages day after tomorrow."

CHAPTER SEVENTEEN

Under the hot lash of the New Mexico sun, Dan Colt rode the big black up the sun-struck main street of Albuquerque. It was midafternoon and the street was active with creaking wagons, a few riders on horseback, and people moving about on foot.

A thin thread of resentment was running through the tall, blond man. Instead of riding close on Dave's heels, he now was forced to abandon that search for a quartet of dastardly deserters. Wicked thoughts lodged in his mind about Colonel Jeffrey Allen. He wondered if Logan Tanner had reached Fort Ryan yet.

As thoughts danced through his brain, Colt pondered on the lovely face of Marla Wells. There was something different about Marla. She wasn't a run-of-the-mill type. She had real character. And *spirit*. He could see her desperate features again, as she held the Derringer on him. There was something in that splendid female . . . something that affected him deep inside.

Unconsciously, Dan's eyes fell on the big sign that read, ALBUQUERQUE BANK AND TRUST. New thoughts crowded out those of Marla Wells. The four deserters had turned to robbing banks. Certainly after successfully cleaning out Socorro's two banks, they would be encouraged to try it again in Albuquerque.

Passing the Blue Chip Casino, Dan noted the unusual number of horses standing hip-shot at the hitching-rail. Business was not ordinarily that good at a casino until after sundown. He thought of his twin. Dave was a sharp hand at poker. *Maybe* . . . Dan shook his head. *No,* he told himself. *If I get sidetracked trying to run down Dave, I'll let Caraway and his bunch get away. Be all right if I caught Dave, then I wouldn't need that affidavit. But if Dave's already been here and gone* . . .

The sheriff's office was coming up on the right. It was always a strain on the nerves for Dan to walk into a lawman's office, but if the deserters had been here, he had to know it. Swinging from the saddle, Dan tied the black at the rail, wishing there was some shade somewhere. A few minutes of that blistering sun on the saddle and it would be too hot to sit in.

Two women passed the tall man on the board sidewalk. They were chattering like a pair of chipmunks and did not look at him. Opening the office door and ducking his head, Dan entered the hot, stuffy room. It was empty. "Anyone here?" he called.

Getting no response, he backed out and closed the door. Suddenly his attention was drawn up the street where a crowd was gathering around a group of weary-looking, bedraggled men who were climbing out of the back of a large wagon. Studying the scene, Dan saw a young man with a badge on his vest come out of the Red Bird Cafe. With haste, he elbowed his way through the crowd. Though obviously dead-tired, the six men all spoke at once, waving their arms wildly.

By listening closely, Colt picked up enough to learn that these men had comprised a posse. Bank robbers had caught them off guard and taken their horses. They asked about a man named Bender and were told that he was going to be all right.

Dan waited in the shade of the office porch until the group dispersed and the young deputy heeled around and headed for the office.

Leon Hatch had his eyes downward as he stepped on the boardwalk. He lifted them just as he reached the door. Smiling, Dan said, "You the law here?"

When Hatch lined on Colt's angular, tanned face, his body flinched. Instinctively his hand dropped for the gun on his hip. Before he could clear the holster, the tall man had palmed both guns, lining the muzzles on the deputy's belly. Hatch swallowed hard, probing Colt's intent features with frightened eyes.

"Wait a minute, deputy," said Dan with a half-smile. "I'm not who you think I am."

The deputy let his gun slide back into the holster. Instantly Dan flipped the twin Colts adeptly and holstered them.

"I know who you are," said Hatch, nervously. "You're *Dan Colt*."

Dan's face muscles slackened. Surprise registered in his sky-blue eyes. This was a switch. Following in the crooked swath cut by his twin, he was accustomed to being mistakenly called Dave Sundeen. "How do you know I'm Dan Colt?"

"You know," snapped the deputy, gaining courage.

"This may sound strange to you, son," said Dan, "but the last time I was in Albuquerque you were carryin' apples to your teacher."

Dan studied the furtive expression of skepticism that formed on Leon Hatch's face.

"It's the truth," breathed Colt.

Hatch swore. "Then who was it that pulled a gun on me and locked me up in that cell yesterday morning? Your *twin brother*?" The sarcasm in the deputy's voice was like an arctic wind.

Dan pushed his hat back from his sweaty brow. "Exactly."

Excitement bolted through Dan Colt like jagged white lightning. He was only one day behind Dave Sundeen!

Hatch's eyes bulged. Anger welled up in him. "You're tellin' me that you ain't the man who gunned down Bobby Braden right over there?" he asked heatedly, pointing to the spot where Braden had died in the street.

"Nope."

Hatch sleeved saliva from his mouth. "And you ain't the dude who robbed all three of our banks with your gang of uniformed bandits?"

The deputy's words came one at a time like sledgehammer blows. They bounced off the walls of Dan's brain, then reverberated through his head, finally settling in his consciousness. Taking hold of Hatch's narrow shoulders, Colt said, "Would you say that one more time?"

"Wh-what?"

"About the uniformed bandits."

Hatch's face twisted in confusion. "Do you really have a twin?"

"Yes," breathed Dan heavily. "Are you tellin' me that he is runnin' with those cavalry deserters? Robbin' banks?"

"Well, if it ain't you, it sure as fire is him!" exclaimed Hatch.

Dan felt like hugging the deputy. This was more than he could hope for. Dave and the Caraway gang traveling together! All he really needed was Dave. But why not take them all? Colonel Allen did say the government would give a reward. If Allen was telling the truth, he would add a nice chunk himself. Funds *had* been running low lately. Dan had not taken time to stop and do some work. Logan Tanner was hot on his heels. It was imperative that he catch Dave soon.

Colt had no plan at the moment as to how he would capture the five men, but he would cross that bridge when it lay at his feet.

"Listen, deputy," said Dan, "do you have any idea where the bank robbers might be headed?"

"They robbed the stage comin' from Santa Fe this mornin'," said Hatch advisedly. "Driver said they were plannin' on headin' for Santa Fe, but he told them that we had wired the law there and warned them. Said they changed their minds. They'd ride another direction."

"He say which way?"

"The bandits didn't say. They loaded up one of the

posse who was shot and told the driver to get him to the doc here in town, *pronto*. Driver said the robber saw this morning's stage heading toward 'em from Albuquerque, so they hurried him off. Wanted to rob the other one, too."

Dan Colt was so elated with the sudden turn of events and so engrossed in his conversation with Leon Hatch that he failed to notice the five men approaching. Suddenly, a big, booming voice said, "Get your hands up, Colt!"

Spinning, Dan found himself facing five shotguns. Henry Byas spoke again. "That was good work, Leon. You kept him talking until we could get the drop on him."

As Colt's hands slid slowly upward, Leon Hatch lifted the twin .45's from their holsters.

Eyeing Byas cautiously, Dan said, "You called me *Colt*. Do I know you?"

Anger flared in Byas's moon-shaped face. "What do you mean, do you know me? I told you the day you shot Bobby Braden that I knew you from Kansas. You stuck a gun in my face yesterday and robbed my bank. What kind of nonsense you tryin' to pull?"

"He's got a slick one cooked up, Mister Byas," said the deputy. "Says the feller that shot Braden and leads them blue bandits is his identical twin!" Hatch broke into a laugh. The others joined in.

"Boy, that's a hot one!" put in another. "Wants us to let him go and hang his twin, I betcha!" The growing crowd laughed again.

"Open the door, Leon," said Byas, "let's get him in a cell."

"Look, mister," said Dan, impatience riding his

voice, "if I had done what you just said, would I come back into town like this?"

"Was a little stupid, Colt. Why'd you do it?"

"'Cause I'm not the one who robbed you, that's why."

"Lead the way, Leon," said Byas, ignoring Dan's statement. "Let's lock him up. We'll have his trial tomorrow . . . hang him the next day. Might even give him an extra day to live if he tells us where the money is."

Dan went mute as he was crowded into the stifling office. The stagnant air seemed to grow hotter as he moved toward the cell area in the rear. The door clanked shut. Hatch turned the key. A wave of despair swept over Dan Colt, erasing the last flicker of the elation he had known only a few moments earlier. Morosely he sagged onto the bunk.

All the men left, including the deputy. The cell was like an overheated oven. Dan removed his hat, tossing it on an upright chair which sat in a corner of his ten-by-ten prison. Standing up, he unbuckled his gun belt, slipped out of his vest, and peeled off his shirt. Stretching out on the bunk, he lay on his back. Bitterness was surging through him like the raging waters of an angry river.

What foul thing in life had he done to deserve this? He had been able to accept Mary's death, brutal as it was. Lots of other men have had their wives murdered. There even had been some compensation. Mary's killers were now in hell . . . sent there by Dan's own hands. But this Sundeen thing was the thorn in his flesh. Falsely arrested and accused. Erroneously convicted. Five months he had languished in that ghastly inferno at Yuma. Then came the good fortune. Circumstances opened the prison gates. He had escaped without hindrance . . . escaped to track down his outlaw twin and clear his own name. But it seemed like an evil, unseen force had dogged his tracks. Every time he was about to close in on Sundeen, the invisible nemesis would raise up a barrier to thwart his success.

As his body moistened with sweat produced by the suffocating heat, Dan Colt entertained the notion of breaking out of this place and heading east. He would leave the West. Leave it for good. Lose himself in Boston or New York. Frontier law would never track him there. Even Logan Tanner would turn around and give up at the west bank of the wide Missouri.

Time crawled slowly. Finally, the blazing sun dropped below the horizon and the long day began its demise. Darkness gradually enveloped the land, cooling the desert. There was no breeze which often came with nightfall. The open window in the cell offered no relief. The heat in the jail seemed trapped, even as was Dan Colt.

With bitterness gnawing at his every fiber, Dan had not thought of his empty stomach or dry throat. Suddenly, he heard the outer door of the office squeak open. The flare of a match cast a momentary glow into the pitch-black building, followed by the brighter glow of a coal-oil lamp.

Leon Hatch appeared before the bars, holding the lantern to eye level. "Getting hungry, Colt?" he asked as Dan sat up, blinking against the light.

"Hadn't noticed it," came the grim reply. Running

his tongue against the roof of his parched mouth, Dan said, "Sure could use some water."

"I'll get you some. Then bring you a meal." Turning to leave, the deputy said, "By the way. The judge says he can't conduct your trial until day after tomorrow. Looks like you get a small reprieve."

"Yeah, looks like it," Colt replied dryly.

After belting down a good meal and getting his fill of water, the tall man settled down in the darkness for the night. He lay on the bunk, trying to figure a way to escape. Slowly, dullness engulfed his brain and he fell asleep.

The next day was uneventful. His meals and other needs were provided for through a small door in the exterior cell wall. There was no way to overpower anyone attending the prisoner. The cell door remained shut.

As night darkened the cell, Dan was beginning to wonder when Hatch would show up with his meal. The outer door opened, and presently a tall, square-shouldered man in his midthirties appeared, followed by Hatch. The latter held a lantern.

"Mister Colt, I'm Sheriff Webb Reber," said the square-shouldered man.

Dan rolled off the bunk and approached the bars.

"I've heard a lot about you, Colt," said Reber. "Understood you were dead. I'd doubt your identity except for the way they tell me you outdrew 'Bad Boy' Braden."

Dan opened his mouth to speak.

Butting in, the sheriff continued, "You sure have changed from the way you used to be." Reber clucked

BANDITS IN BLUE

his tongue, wagging his head. "A man of your stature lowering himself to robbing banks."

"Sheriff, there's an explanation to this, if you'll just listen."

"I've already heard the twin-brother story," said Reber, his face taking on a slanted, skeptical look. "I'm not buying it."

"I know it sounds farfetched," said Dan imploringly, "but will you let *me* tell it to you?"

"Waste of my time and your breath," snapped Reber. "I have too many witnesses to the contrary. Besides that, Henry Byas says he knows you from Kansas. Says you're the man who robbed his bank."

"Then how about riding south with me to Fort Ryan?"

"What for?"

"The commanding officer there has positive proof of the existence of my identical twin . . . and that he was right there at the fort several days ago."

"If I rode out of this town with you, your gang would ambush me and ride away with you."

"Then send someone to get testimony from Colonel Allen. I'm on an errand for him. He'll gladly produce the evidence you need when he finds out I'm being detained."

A hardness came over Webb Reber's features. "I'm doing no such thing, Colt. There's Indian trouble down that way right now and you know it. You're just trying to stall things and buy time."

Dan gripped the bars, his knuckles whitening. "Is there no one in this world who will look a man in the eye and say *'maybe he's telling the truth'*?"

"Every criminal I've ever put behind bars was lily-white and innocent, Colt. Just ask them."

Anger whipped through Dan Colt like a high-winded prairie fire. Too many undeserved atrocities had been leveled against him. Too much pressure had gone unrelieved for too long.

In blind fury, the muscular Colt flashed a hand through the bars, sinking spring-steel fingers into Reber's shirt. Recoiling his arm, he slammed the sheriff's face savagely into the bars. As the dazed Reber strained to free himself, Dan reached through the bars and grabbed his gun.

Stunned at first by Dan's action, Leon Hatch stood frozen, mouth gaping. Suddenly, he wheeled, leaving the two men in the darkness. He could be heard running up the street, crying for help.

Holding Reber's face solidly to the bars with one hand and the revolver in the other, Colt said, "Let's have the keys."

Grimacing in pain, the sheriff said, "They're out in the office."

A cold stream like ice water flowed next to Dan's spine. Reber was no doubt telling the truth. He had not come to unlock the cell. He would have no reason to carry the keys. If Dan let the man go, he would be free to slip away in the dark. Within minutes the place was going to be swarming with armed men. His burst of temper resulting in overpowering Reber and getting his gun was to no avail.

Possibly with all six bullets he could destroy the lock on the cell door. He would have to hit the latch dead-center. That would be impossible in the darkness.

Heavy footsteps were now thundering on the boardwalk outside.

Realizing that Dan was considering the hopeless situation, Reber said, "It'll go better for you if I have that gun back before those men come charging in here." His face was still welded to the bars. "I know you can hold the gun to my head and threaten to kill me, but Dan Colt is not a cold-blooded killer. You have changed, but not that much." Reber paused. "Or have you?"

The sheriff felt the pressure ease. Dan's fingers released the shirt. Reber felt the sweaty grips of the revolver touch his hand through the bars. Suddenly the office was overrun with lantern-bearing armed men. Sheriff Webb Reber stepped out of the dark corridor to meet them. "It's all right, men," he said calmly. "The danger's over. Mister Colt gave me back my gun."

Henry Byas eyed the vertical red welts on Reber's face. "Looks like he tried to put your head through the bars."

Reber touched the bruises tenderly with his fingertips. A wry smile moved across his lips. "Felt to me like he was gonna pull the bars through my head."

CHAPTER EIGHTEEN

Dan Colt sat down on the bunk, his anger rapidly cooling. The office cleared out within a few moments. Everybody was gone, including the two lawmen. They had left a lantern burning on the desk. The soft glow of light filtered into the cell area.

Dan pondered the fracas. He was surprised that Reber had taken his roughing up so well . . . had not retaliated in anger.

Some thirty minutes after the office had cleared, Reber and Hatch returned. As they entered the cell area, the aroma of hot food and steaming coffee met Dan's nostrils. The tall, square-shouldered sheriff unlocked the cell door and swung it open. The young deputy carried the tray inside the cell and placed it on the small table.

"Thought you might be getting hungry, Colt," said Reber. "I sure am. If you don't mind, you and I will dine together." Hatch retraced his steps and walked into the office. Reber closed and locked the cell door. "Well . . . *almost* together," he said.

Leon Hatch returned carrying a small table, much like the one in Dan's cell. Placing it next to the bars, he left again.

"You don't mind, do you, Colt?" asked the sheriff.

"No," said the blond-headed prisoner. "Not at all."

"Good," said Reber, as Hatch reappeared, carrying a straight-backed chair. Once again the deputy disappeared. "I want to talk to you," added Reber.

A bit perplexed, Dan said, "Okay by me."

Hatch reappeared again carrying a tray identical to Dan's.

"Thanks, Leon," said Webb Reber. "You can go now."

"G'nite," offered Leon, passing through the door.

As the deputy's footsteps were fading away, Reber turned his face toward the door. "Leon!"

"Yessir," came the distant reply.

"Just leave the front door open. Maybe a breeze will come along."

"Yessir," answered Hatch and was gone.

Sitting down and scraping the chair up to the table, the sheriff said, "Colt, why don't you pull your table over here by the door? Bring that chair over and it'll almost be like we're sitting at the same table."

Puzzled, Dan began shifting furniture. While he did so, Reber eyed the lantern sitting on the floor behind him. Getting out of the chair, he picked up the lantern and hung it on a piece of heavy wire directly overhead. "There," he said, looking at Dan, "now the light will be better."

As the two men dug into the food, Webb Reber spoke around a mouthful of potatoes, "Look, Colt, I'm sorry about the way I treated you awhile ago..."

Dan eyed him cautiously.

"I mean for not letting you tell your side of the story," Reber said, swallowing.

"I'm sorry I roughed you up," said Dan, responding readily to the lawman's apology. "I shouldn't have slammed you so hard."

"Yes you should've," said Webb, smiling. "You knocked a little sense into my head. Made me think about what you said."

"What's that?" asked Dan, taking a gulp of coffee.

"That part about looking a man in the eye and figuring maybe he's telling the truth."

"Mmm-hmm," said Dan, chewing. His pale blue eyes were riveted on Reber's face.

"My old daddy used to say you can read a man through his eyes. While you were pressing my face against the bars, I thought of one time when my old daddy was gonna whip me for something I hadn't done. It appeared that I was guilty, but I wasn't. I thought sure he was gonna whale the daylights out of me. He was pulling off his big broad belt in spite of my protesting words of innocence. Just before he cut loose, he said, 'Son, look me square in the eye and tell me you didn't do it.' I was glad to. As I did, he read me close and decided I was telling the truth."

"Mmm-hmm," said Dan. "Now you want to read me?"

"Yeah. I want you to tell me your story, looking me square in the eye."

"Gladly," said the blue-eyed prisoner. He began with Mary's murder and within less than an hour, had brought Sheriff Webb Reber up to the present moment.

Reber sloshed the coffee in his cup and shook his head. "That's some story, Dan," he said. "Some story."

"Well?" said Colt, studying the lawman's gray eyes.

"That's some story."

"You think I'm lyin'." Dan's lips were drawn tight.

"By every indication," said Reber, "you're telling me the truth."

"Just ride with me to Ryan and you won't have to depend on my eyes."

"The judge has got your trial set for tomorrow afternoon," said the sheriff. "The only thing I can do now is try to get it postponed." Standing up, he looked at Dan warmly. "I'll see him first thing in the morning."

Rising to his full height, Dan said, "Then you *will* ride with me to Fort Ryan?"

"Yessir," replied Webb, smiling broadly. "I'll just do that."

Hope was once again ignited in Dan Colt's heart. Certainly Colonel Allen would produce the affidavit if it meant getting him released to continue his pursuit of Caraway's gang.

A slight breeze moved through the jail. Dan settled down on the bunk as the sheriff bid him good night and doused the light. He lay in the dark enjoying the breeze. The face of Marla Wells drifted into his mind. Why did he keep thinking of Marla? Dan told himself it was because of her plight. He felt sorry for her. Apparently she was like himself. She had lost the one she loved . . . and she had no family. Like Dan, Marla was alone. That's why she so often came to mind. By personal experience, he related to her sorrow.

Within a few minutes he was asleep.

Sheriff Webb Reber came with a breakfast tray at six thirty. Before leaving, he said, "I'll see the judge at nine, Dan. If he grants the postponement, we'll be on the road to Fort Ryan by ten o'clock."

"You think there'll be a problem?" asked Colt, blowing on the steaming coffee.

"Shouldn't be. I'll explain that it could mean important evidence regarding the trial."

"I'll be ready," said Dan with a tight smile. "All I have to do is shave and comb my hair."

"See you later." Reber turned to leave.

"Sheriff," said Dan.

"Yeah?"

"Thanks for listenin'."

Webb Reber smiled blandly and disappeared through the door.

Time seemed to drag. Through the cell window, Dan watched the world grow lighter. He thought about the fort. The colonel. The Comanches. He hope the hostilities had subsided.

As he soaped his face with cool water and shaved, his thoughts drifted back to the Wyoming ranch. He remembered how Mary would stand at an angle behind him when he shaved, so he could see her in the mirror. As his eyes would drift from his own lathered face to hers, she would silently mouth the words *I love you*. A sharp pang of loneliness ran through him.

Splashing water in his face to remove the remaining soap, Dan thought of Marla. He wondered how long she would stay in Socorro. That one-horse town was no place for a lady of her caliber to settle down.

The morning wore on. Picking up his vest, Dan fished in the left-hand pocket for his watch. It had stopped. He had forgotten to wind it. Stepping to the small barred window, he checked the angle of the shadow outside. *Must be at least ten o'clock,* he thought to himself. *Where's Reber? Maybe the judge wouldn't listen. Maybe—*

The sound of rapid footsteps met Dan's ears. At first they were on the boardwalk outside, then in the office. Abruptly, Webb Reber appeared, followed by two dust-covered, scraggly-looking men.

Dan approached the bars.

"Take a good look," Reber said to the two men, fixing his own gaze on Dan's rugged features.

Art Cadwell stared at Dan Colt with unbelieving eyes. He swallowed hard. His sharp, protruding Adam's apple dropped, then bobbed back into place. His mouth hung open.

Percy Smythe swore, his eyes wide.

"Whaddya say, boys?" asked the sheriff, impatiently.

"It's ... it's ... it's *him!*" gulped Cadwell.

Smythe swore again, blinked, and rubbed his eyes. Dan waited silently.

"You agree, Percy?" demanded Reber.

"Not a doubt in the world," replied Smythe. "It's him ... but ... but it *ain't* him."

"Why do you say that?" Webb Reber asked, a broad smile capturing his lips.

"Cuz it ain't possible," said Smythe, eyes still bulging.

Webb gave Dan a confident look, then swung his gaze back to the shotgunner. "Why?"

"You said this feller's been locked up right here for two days?"

"That's right."

Art Cadwell stood mute and staring as Percy Smythe said, "We wuz held up fer the second time by them cavalry troopers less than an hour ago. The leader of that pack o' wolves had the same face as this feller!"

Dan Colt's heart was pounding like a runaway trip-hammer. Joy was escalating through him in waves.

Unlocking the door and swinging it wide, Reber said, "Dan, we all owe you a big apology. Get your things. You're a free man!"

By noon, Dan Colt had strapped on his guns, procured the big black gelding, and was sitting at a table in the Red Bird Cafe. Facing him across the table was Sheriff Webb Reber. As a gesture of good faith, the tall, square-shouldered lawman had bought him the biggest steak on the menu with all the trimmings.

"Dan, I think I've learned a good lesson in all of this," said Reber.

"Mmm?" said Colt, chewing heartily.

"A good law officer has to be tough, yes. He has to be firm. But he still must have room in his makeup for compassion."

"Mmm-hmm," agreed the blond man, still chewing. Swallowing, he smacked his lips. As he mopped gravy across his plate with a chunk of bread, Dan said, "My dad . . . that is, Ben Mason, who raised me . . . once showed me in the Bible that a law officer is like a preacher."

"Yeah?"

"Mmm-hmm. Preacher has to be tough against sin and firm on wrong-doin'. But he also has to keep a tender spot for the people he deals with."

Webb Reber smiled, exposing a mouthful of teeth. "That's pretty straight thinking, Dan. I'll do my best to remember it."

Dan was draining the last of his coffee.

"I still think you ought to let me round up some men and let us help you catch these culprits," the sheriff said with insistence. "You know, with all these stage holdups, Wells Fargo is going to bring in their own posse."

"One man has a better chance of sneakin' up on 'em," said Colt flatly. "I can have 'em in custody before Wells Fargo can turn a hand."

"One thing for sure," said Reber, "until we can find and repair all the breaks in the telegraph lines, nobody's going to get ahold of anybody. We can't get a message out in either direction."

"Yep," agreed Dan, "they'll be long gone before anybody can organize against them."

"You have a plan how you're going to take them?"

"Nope. I'll just have to play it by ear. I'll figure a way once I find 'em."

The sheriff eyed Colt with caution. "I have a plan. Will you at least listen?"

Dan motioned to the waitress, holding up his empty coffee cup. "All right. You finally listened to me. Guess I can listen to you. Fire away."

As the waitress filled both coffee cups, Webb said, "Instead of beating the bushes looking for them ... why don't you make *them* come to you?"

"I'm still listenin'."

"Three days ago when your brother and his gang held up Cadwell's stage, he and Smythe told them that we had gotten a message through to the sheriff at Raton about the banks being robbed here. The gang argued that it couldn't be. They had cut the wires on their way out of town. Cadwell insisted the message was sent and acknowledged just before the wires were cut."

"They buy it?"

"Art says they were skeptical, but unsure. Evidence is clear they didn't feel safe about it. They're hanging around about fifteen miles north of here, just robbing all the stages that pass through."

Sipping from the steaming cup, Dan said, "I'm still listenin'."

"Maybe they are out there waiting for another stage. We can take them one. They'll come right to us."

Dan Colt's face brightened. "Hey, you're pretty smart for a fella that wears a badge. I'm warmin' up to the idea. Go ahead."

Reber's face clouded. "Well uh ... uh, that's as

BANDITS IN BLUE

far as my plan has developed." Grinning ardently, he said, "But you got to admit, the idea has merit!"

Capitalizing on Webb's idea, Dan's own plan began to formulate. "Yep, that it does." Leaning across the table supported by his elbows, Dan said, "Can we talk to the driver and gunner... what's their names?"

"Driver's Art Cadwell. Gunner's Percy Smythe."

"Would their stage be free to turn around and head back toward Santa Fe?"

"I think they've already pulled out for Socorro. Should've. Was supposed to leave thirty minutes ago." Standing up, Reber walked to the door and stepped out on the boardwalk. Wheeling, he returned. "It's gone."

As Reber sat down, Dan said, "When's the next one due?"

"There will be one back from Las Cruces day after tomorrow."

Shaking his head and gritting his teeth, Colt said, "Can't wait that long."

"There's a spare stagecoach out in the alley behind the Fargo office," offered Reber. "There's always a team of Fargo horses at the Big Pine Corral." The sheriff's brow furrowed. "But, Dan, if we take a stage north ahead of time... won't the robbers get suspicious? They must know the schedule."

"On the contrary," said the tall, blond man. "With all the holdups, it would look like we were dodging the schedule to try to get through without being robbed."

Webb's face grew thoughtful. "Makes sense."

"We could load it with boxes. Make it look like a cargo haul. That way we wouldn't have to carry any passengers. Got a couple men in town who could go as driver and shotgunner?"

"I can drive it," said Reber. "I'll get Hugo Hogan to ride shotgun. He used to work for Fargo doing just that. Where'll you be?"

"I figure to load some trunks and crates up on top," said Dan. "I'll lay down between them. When you think they're positioned just right, give me a word signal and I'll pop up with both guns. They'll no doubt make you two throw your guns on the ground. You need to have a couple revolvers stashed on the floorboard."

"Sounds good," smiled the sheriff.

"Wish I knew what kind of an approach they use," mused Dan. "We'd know better how to plan."

"We could talk to the passenger they shot this morning," said Reber. "If he's still alive."

Dan's eyes widened. "They shot a passenger."

"Yeah. Art said the man merely moved his hand. Passengers were lined up outside the coach, hands in the air. Art said the man moved his hand to wipe sweat from his face. Tall, yellow-haired fella wearin' sergeant's stripes shot him."

"Caraway," breathed Dan. "At least I hope it wasn't Dave."

The two tall men left the Red Bird and hurried to the doctor's office. To their dismay, they found that the wounded Wells Fargo passenger had died. They stepped out into the bright sunlight.

"You'll just have to watch them approach, act like you're talking to Hugo, and tell me how they're lining up," said Dan. "When they get close and it looks good, give me the signal and I'll jump up and get the drop on 'em."

"I just had a horrible thought," said Webb with a worried look.

"What's that?"

"What if we go to all this trouble and they don't take the bait?"

Dan chuckled. "Then I guess we get a nice joyride to Santa Fe." Clapping a hand on Reber's shoulder, he said, "I have a strong feelin' they'll show up, all right. Let's get going. I want to deliver those four deserters to Colonel Allen . . . and my brother to Logan Tanner."

CHAPTER NINETEEN

Joe Caraway dismounted as the gang returned to the wooded camp in the Sandia Mountains. As the others eased their way out of the saddles, Dave Sundeen sprang from his own saddle and stomped toward Caraway, who was loosening his cinch.

Sundeen sank his fingers into Caraway's shoulder, spun him around, and sent a savage punch to his nose. Joe went down hard as his horse shied, ejecting a shrill whinny. Dave stood spread-legged over him. "You had no call to shoot that man!" he bellowed.

Caraway rolled over and raised to his knees. The world was spinning as he looked up at the tall, muscular man through watery eyes. Blood spurted from his nose.

"All he was doin' was wipin' sweat from his face," continued Sundeen.

"I thought he was gonna reach for a gun, Dave," said Caraway, protesting.

Sundeen reached down, clutched his shirt, and lifted Joe to his feet. Holding him erect and eye-to-eye, he said, "Where did you think he had the gun? In his ear? Under his hat?"

The other bandits looked on in helpless consternation as Sundeen shook Joe hard, snapping his neck. "That man will probably die," said Dave through clenched teeth. "And for what? Bein' scared? Moppin' sweat?" Cocking the arm that held the bleeding Caraway, Dave gave him a hard shove. The ex-sergeant stumbled and fell to the ground. As he lay there wiping blood from his nose, Sundeen walked to his own horse and removed the McClellan saddle.

Dropping the saddle to the ground, he turned to the others, who stood in silence. "One of you boys better get up on the lookout point. Could be a posse come this way just any time."

"I'll go," said Alex Hopper.

The others left Joe Caraway to stop his nosebleed and went about unsaddling their horses.

The camp was situated about fifty yards into the forest on the west edge of the rugged Sandias. Jutting straight skyward from the forest floor was a vertical rock formation. It was jagged enough to be easily ascended. The formation was some seventy feet in circumference at its base and tapered to about twenty feet at the top. It was almost flat on the summit, which towered nearly eighty feet in the air.

Alex Hopper was glad to remove himself from the others. The tension was tight when Dave Sundeen was angry. Quickly, he scrambled his way to the lofty pinnacle of the rock and sat down. He cast a quick glance to the west, then south toward Albuquerque.

Morgan Hill

Then north toward Santa Fe. The land lay motionless and undisturbed in the harsh light of the sun.

Hopper removed his hat and mopped his brow with a bandanna. A slight breeze plucked at his hair. Looking down at Joe Caraway, who was now seated on a fallen tree nursing his nose, Alex wondered what Sundeen would do to Joe if he knew that the man had lied about not killing any troopers the day they deserted.

The afternoon sun was beginning to slant downward when Sundeen, Deere, and Stevens were checking the loot from the morning's stage robbery. They sat in a semicircle on a bed of pine needles, when suddenly Alex Hopper's voice cut the hot air. "Dave! Stage comin' from Albuquerque!"

Joe Caraway, still sitting moodily on the fallen tree, lifted his head.

Standing to his feet, Sundeen squinted toward Hopper's lofty perch. "Can't be, Alex! There's no stage due from that direction for a couple days!"

"Well, it *is*!" came the positive reply.

"Come on down!" shouted Dave. As Joe Caraway walked toward them, Sundeen said, "They're pullin' a fast one on us, boys. Trying to sneak one through to Santa Fe. Saddle up!"

Dan Colt lay belly-down on top of the bounding stage, wishing he had thought to bring along some pillows. If this ride lasted long, he would have to have his ribs and stomach put back in place.

Empty trunks and wooden cartons had been nailed to the top of the stage, surrounding him. Ropes were lashed to them to give the appearance that they were tied to the metal rack. A slight opening was left between the trunks to the forward right and left, giving him at least a partial view of the ground.

In the passenger area below were piles of empty cardboard boxes. On the seat just ahead were Webb Reber and Hugo Hogan. Hogan was in his early seventies, having recently retired as a Wells Fargo shotgunner. Reber held the reins, seated to Dan's left. Hogan cradled the single-barrel twelve gauge, seated to the right.

As the stagecoach bumped along, Dan thought of his short-lived plan to go east and lose himself in one of the big cities. Smiling to himself, he pondered the foolishness of such an idea. He was born for the wide open spaces. To live in a cramped and crowded city would kill him for sure. No, he would take his chances in this wide and rugged country.

Suddenly, as he adjusted his position, it came to his mind. *This could be the day I capture Dave and end the horrible nightmare.* Chances were mighty good that soon his name would be cleared and he could return to a normal life. Whatever that is.

Dan Colt had actually given very little thought to what he would do once he had the law off his back. Mary was gone. He loved ranching . . . when he shared the life with Mary. What did he have now? Nothing.

The lovely face of Marla Wells glided into his thoughts when Webb Reber's voice intruded brusquely, "We're nearing the general area where the holdups have been, Dan!"

Removing his hat, Dan lifted his head to look at Reber. "Okay!" he hollered. "You two keep your eyes peeled!" Edging up closer to Hugo Hogan, he said loudly, "You're sure you remember the signal to reach down and grab that gun on the floor?"

"Yep! Just like we planned," said Hugo in his usual crackly voice. "When Webb sees they're in the best position, he'll say, 'We're not carrying anything of value.' When he says that, you'll pop up with both guns and I'm to go for this'n on the floor!"

Listening hard, Webb Reber nodded in agreement, and Dan said, "That's it, Hugo!"

Suddenly Reber caught sight of movement off to the right. Narrowing his eyes against the desert's glare, he saw five men in blue riding hard in a straight course to intercept them.

"Here they come, Dan!" he shouted.

"How far away?" came the voice from between the trunks.

"They'll stop us in less than two minutes!"

Dan's heart jumped to his throat. In less than two minutes he would lay eyes on his brother whom he had not seen in thirty years. An abrupt sadness washed over him. *Oh, Dave. Why did it have to be like this? You're the only kin I have in this whole world. If only you weren't an outlaw . . . if only we were free to ride the West together. If only . . .*

Turning his head as if speaking to Hogan, Reber said, "About one minute, now, Dan! They're fanning out. Looks like there'll be one in front, two on each side. If I clear my throat, you'll know there's one goes to the rear. Okay?"

"Okay!" Dan's breath was coming in short gulps, now. He thought of what a shock Dave was going to get when he saw his twin brother's face.

The stage was slowing down.

Colt felt his whole body throbbing. A cool trickle of sweat rolled down his back. As the traces rattled, the vehicle rolled to a stop. Poised, with both guns ready, Dan waited.

"Good afternoon, gentlemen," came a voice that held a familiar ring. "This is a robbery. Now driver, you toss your sidearm to the ground, and gunner, you do the same with the big one."

As the guns clattered to the ground and the bandits were carefully observing the top-heavy coach and box-filled passenger compartment, Dan peered through the opening on the right side. He did not recognize either man. Shifting to the other side, the first face was unfamiliar. But the second ...

Cold chills swept over him. His blood went from hot to cold to hot. The sensation was indescribable. It was like looking at himself from outside his body. *Identical!* No wonder Logan Tanner was impossible to convince!

Dan's frame trembled and perspired. Joe Caraway must be the one directly in front. None of the others fit the description.

It had been Dave who spoke before. He spoke again. "Isn't this stage off schedule, gentlemen?"

As Webb Reber said, "This is a special cargo shipment," Dan fixed his gaze on his brother. He could shoot Dave from this very spot. No matter what happened to the others, he would have Dave's body to show Logan Tanner. No more threat of Yuma. No more lonely trails. No more looking over his shoulder, dodging the law. No more riding into towns on

Morgan Hill

Dave's heels and taking the brunt for his deeds. Just one squeeze of the trigger ...

Dan Colt shook himself. *No way,* he thought. *I can't kill my own brother. Got to take him alive. Wing him if he resists ... but alive.*

Dan waited, ready to strike like an uncoiling rattler.

Webb Reber eyed the positions of the five men. The long, lanky sergeant sat his horse straight in front of them, gun in hand. The others were spread evenly, forming almost a perfect half-circle. They would never be positioned any better. He must give the signal *now*.

Reber opened his mouth to speak. Before he could get the first word of the signal out, Dave Sundeen edged his horse forward, saying, "You two climb down."

Dan knew if Reber and Hogan left the seat, they couldn't get to the guns. He listened intently.

Both men on the seat were thinking the same thing. It was now or never. Hugo's nerves were strung tight. Reber spoke quickly. "We're not carrying—"

Hugo dove for the gun at his feet before Dan could be sure he was actually getting the signal. Joe Caraway's revolver belched fire. As Hugo took the bullet and peeled over the side, the startled team bolted. Sundeen's horse reared and wheeled with fright, as the coach lunged forward. Webb Reber, caught off balance, fell hard to the ground. Rolling in the dust, he grasped his gun, which lay in arm's reach.

Dan raised up on the coach, just as Ken Deere fired and hit Reber. Taking aim as best he could on the bounding vehicle, Dan let go with both guns. Deere stiffened and toppled from his horse. Alex Hopper, who was directly behind Deere, caught a bullet in the head and plunged earthward.

No one had a good look at Dan's face. Least of all, Dave Sundeen, whose horse had turned completely around. The frightened team soon carried the stage out of pistol range. Joe Caraway took one look at Deere and Hopper sprawled on the ground and said, "Let's get out of here!"

Dave Sundeen eyed the crumpled forms of Reber and Hogan. "I'm pullin' out," he said. "You two can have the stuff at the camp. This game is over!"

Joe Caraway swore at Sundeen as he galloped away heading due south. Turning to Frank Stevens, he said, "Let's head for the camp!"

As Caraway and Stevens raked their horses' sides and headed eastward, Webb Reber slowly rolled over and lifted his head. Trying to clear his vision, he watched the vague forms of the two bandits fade from sight. Deere's bullet had hit him in the left shoulder and passed through, missing the bone.

Slowly, the wounded sheriff gained his feet and staggered to Hugo. The old shotgunner was dead. Deere and Hopper were also dead. Their horses stood nearby.

Dropping weakly to his knees, Reber lifted his gaze to the north. Dan Colt had gained control of the runaway team and was coming back as fast as he had left. Resting on his haunches, the bleeding sheriff watched the weaving stagecoach slide to a stop in a cloud of dust. Colt leaped to the ground and ran to

Morgan Hill

Reber, who clutched his wounded shoulder. Blood was running between his fingers.

"How bad is it?" asked Dan, going down on one knee.

"Bullet went clear through," replied Reber, his face twisted with pain.

"I've got to make some kind of a compress," said Dan. "Got to stop that bleeding."

Moments later the compress was in place, made from a clean shirt Dan had found in Alex Hopper's saddlebags. Lifting the sheriff to his feet, the blond man said, "Now let's get you into the coach and head for Albuquerque. I'll toss those empty boxes out and make you comfortable inside."

As they moved toward the stagecoach, Dan cast a longing look at the desert. Dave was gone. A deep, sinking feeling descended on him.

Leaning Reber against a wheel, Dan flung open the door and began pulling boxes from the coach. "Look, Dan," said Webb, "why don't you go after the others?"

Pausing with a box in one hand, Colt said, "And leave you here?"

"I can drive the coach to town. It's not that far."

"Webb, it'll take you close to an hour. You'd never make it. I can't let you try it."

Laying a hand on Colt's muscular shoulder, the sheriff said, "You almost had your brother. He and the other two can't be too far away yet. Go after him, Dan."

Tossing out the last box, Dan eyed Reber closely. "You really think you can make it?"

BANDITS IN BLUE

"Sure I can," said Webb, forcing an optimistic tone into his voice.

"All right," said Dan. "Let me boost you up on the seat. I'll toss those bodies in the coach and tie one of the horses to the rear. You head straight for the doctor when you hit town, understand?"

"Yessir."

"Leave the bodies of the two bandits with the undertaker. I've got to take them with me to the fort."

"Okay."

"Did you see which direction they went?"

"East. Toward the mountains. Must be camped in there."

Within five minutes, the coach was ready to roll. Mounted on Ken Deere's horse, Dan said, "Thanks, Webb. You be careful."

"Good luck, Dan. You bring Dave into Albuquerque. We'll hold him there and you can go after Tanner."

"Sounds great. See you later."

As soon as the stagecoach was moving, Dan raked the horse's sides and galloped toward the mountains.

CHAPTER TWENTY

The sun was dipping low, throwing a long shadow eastward from the towering rock near the bandit camp. Worry gripped Dan Colt as he dismounted at the edge of the forest. In tracking the bandits to this spot, he saw evidence of only two horses. Where had the third man gone? Webb had seen all three men ride this way. Or had he? The wounded sheriff may not have been seeing clearly.

Winding his way quietly and cautiously through the trees, Dan spotted two cavalry horses picketed beside the camp. In the shadow of the tall rock, one man was chopping firewood with a hatchet. He was one that Dan had seen earlier. The other one would have to be either Dave, or Joe Caraway.

Creeping closer, Dan edged up behind a large pine. It was dangerous to try taking one man without knowing where his partner was. Several moments passed. No sign of the other man. The sunlight was fading.

Can't wait, Dan told himself. *Have to take this one now.*

Charging with a tiptoe run, Dan came up behind Frank Stevens, who was still chopping wood. Instinctively, Stevens jerked around as Dan drew within ten feet, guns drawn. Fright and impulse coupled together within Stevens, causing him to suddenly fling the hatchet at Dan Colt. As the tall man dodged the deadly weapon, his guns roared. Stevens toppled backward over a fallen tree.

At that instant Joe Caraway was descending the towering rock. He was about twenty feet from the ground. Hearing the hammer of Caraway's revolver being dogged back, Dan leaped sideways in time to let the bullet sing by. His own bullet scattered rock near Joe's head. The dissident sergeant wheeled and scrambled up the rock. As Dan reached its base, Caraway's gun roared again. Colt flattened himself against the hard surface as the bullet struck rock and whined away angrily.

Inching around until he could see the jagged natural staircase, Dan eyed the spot where Caraway had been. The man was climbing higher. Holstering his left-hand gun, Dan started upward, using his free hand for support and balance.

From higher up Caraway fired again. The booming sound echoed across the rugged mountains.

As Dan continued climbing, the sergeant's voice rang out from overhead, "Dave! It wasn't me that did it! Where'd you get those clothes?"

Dan remained silent, pausing where he stood.

235

"Dave!"

Silence.

"Dave, it wasn't me who took the money from your saddlebags! It . . . it was Hopper. Yeah, it was Hopper!"

Silence.

"Dave! Killin' me won't get your money back. Hopper took it. Please, Dave!"

Dan decided to let the man think he was Dave Sundeen. It was evident Caraway held a fearsome respect for Dan's outlaw twin.

A cluster of small rocks rattled and cascaded down upon Colt. The deserter was climbing higher. Dan thought of Colonel Allen . . . the affidavit . . . Logan Tanner. Maybe it wasn't in the books for Dan to capture his brother. Maybe it would be Tanner's task, after he got a look at the affidavit. Time was wasting. Caraway was the last of the gang. The others were dead. Joe could go to Fort Ryan draped over his horse like the others, or sitting in the saddle. But he *was* going.

Tilting his head back and looking up the craggy rock, Dan saw Joe's face over the tip of a small ledge. The gun muzzle suddenly appeared. Colt slammed himself against the flinty surface as the gun roared. The bullet ricocheted off a slab of stone six inches from his head and screamed away violently.

Again Caraway was climbing, sending stones and fragments downward. Colt came in steady pursuit.

Abruptly, Joe's voice pierced the cooling air. "Dave! You come any higher, I'll kill you!"

"Give it up, Joe!" cried Dan. "I don't want to kill you. I just want to talk to you!"

"You're lyin'!" There was a tremor in Caraway's voice.

As Colt climbed further, he could hear the deserter's boots scraping rock. The gun overhead spit fire again. Dan observed that Caraway was nearing the top. The man had not had time to reload the revolver. He had been too busy scaling the rock. How many times had he fired? Four? Five? One thing for sure. He dared not allow him time to reload.

Reaching the top and gasping for breath, Joe Caraway eyed the dying sun on the western horizon. Wheeling around, he peered over the precipice from the dizzy height. Dan Colt was coming on, grim as death.

"I'm on top, now, Dave!" shouted Caraway. "I have the advantage! Stop, or I'll kill you!"

The brim of Dan's hat appeared briefly, some ten feet below. The revolver bucked against Joe's hand, the shot chipping rock below. Instantly, Colt sprang upward.

Caraway backtracked across the small flat area, stopping with his heels less than a yard from the sheer edge. Spreading his feet, he set himself. Cupping both hands on the revolver, he lined the muzzle on Dan Colt. Before he could pull the trigger, Dan's .45 belched fire.

The slug caught Joe in the belly, buckling him forward. The hammer of his gun snapped hollowly on an empty cartridge. He stood wide-eyed, swaying for a brief instant, then peeled backward over the precipice. His body fell sixty feet before it slammed violently against the tapered rock, then bounced outward, arms and legs flopping like a soggy rag doll.

The skull split open on a sharp rock, splattering blood in every direction. The lifeless form did one more flip, then came to rest at the rough foot of the rock.

As the full moon lifted its orange rim over the earth's edge, Dan Colt rode past the spot where earlier in the day he had seen his twin for the first time in thirty years. Two horses followed on lead ropes, bearing the bodies of Frank Stevens and Joe Caraway.

The memory of Dave Sundeen sitting straight-backed and tall in the McClellan saddle hung in Dan's mind. The same bizarre emotion which he had experienced upon seeing his twin was on him again. As it passed, it left the tall man with an empty, desolate feeling.

Why did life have to jam so many bitter pills down his throat? How much had he and Dave missed out on because of being separated as small boys? It was a strange thing to look at a man he did not even know . . . and yet to love him. Yes, without question, the unnamed sensation which stirred deep within him was a strong, natural love for his brother. But there was more to it than that. There was a curious bond that extended beyond normal brotherly love.

A tight smile worked its way across Dan Colt's face. *Twins.* Of course. That was it. Twins were formed by the hand of God in a mother's womb in a way unlike single births. Suddenly there was a yearning in Dan's heart that he had not known before. Seeing his twin had given birth to a longing strange and new within him. They must meet, become acquainted. He wanted

Dave to know that his twin existed ... to feel the same way.

One thing Dan concluded at that moonlit moment. Logan Tanner would not pursue Dave Sundeen alone. Dan would ride with him. Dave must not die. He must be captured alive. Even when he went to prison, Dan would visit him often. They must become acquainted. Make up for lost time.

As the moon lifted, turning from orange to silver, Dan tossed a glance at the horses that followed. Looking at the lifeless forms dangling over the saddles a thought struck him. The affidavit was not necessary! *Anyone who had seen both twins at the same time could swear to Dave's existence.* There was one man on earth who could do that. *Webb Reber.*

A plan formed in Dan Colt's mind. He should reach Albuquerque before daylight. He would sleep a couple of hours, then ride south. He would find Logan Tanner and bring him to Albuquerque. Reber could tell him what he saw. The army could send a wagon to pick up the bodies of the deserters.

With that settled, Dan set his face toward Albuquerque. *First things first,* he told himself.

It was near midnight when the lone rider leading the two cavalry horses topped a gradual rise and stared into a moonlit wash. He could not believe his eyes. There stood the stagecoach, somber and still in the silver light. One of the horses in the team nickered, followed by another. The bay gelding under Dan Colt answered softly.

Drawing near, Dan's gaze fell to the inert form lying on the ground near the rear of the coach. Bounding from the saddle, he knelt beside the cold, stiff body of Webb Reber. There was a large dark spot where blood had soaked into the sand. Evidence was sufficient. Reber had apparently passed out and fallen from the stagecoach. The impact of the fall had opened the wound. Before he could regain consciousness, he had bled to death.

A cloud moved in front of the moon, bringing a darkness to the desert like the darkness that Dan Colt felt in his soul at that moment. This morning Webb Reber and Hugo Hogan had both laid eyes on Dave Sundeen while Dan crouched behind them on top of the stagecoach. Two men had seen the twins at the same moment. Now they were both dead.

Dan placed Reber's body inside the coach with the other three, then tied the saddle horses, including Deere's bay, to the rear of the stagecoach. Setting a trotting pace, he drove the stage toward town.

Once again, Dan Colt was totally dependent on the affidavit in the hands of Colonel Jeffrey Allen. He resigned himself to it. He would have to take the bodies of the deserters to Fort Ryan. Now there was no—

Wait a minute! There are two other men who can give absolute testimony that twins exist! Art Cadwell and Percy Smythe. Sure, Dan said to himself, *they knew it the minute Reber walked them into that jail!*

The moon had sailed high and distant in the western sky when Dan pulled into Albuquerque. He roused the undertaker out of bed so he could take charge of the bodies, awakened the hostler at the Big Pine Corral for the sake of the horses, then stretched out on the sofa in the lobby of the Sandia Hotel.

At sunup, the tall man belted down a good break-

BANDITS IN BLUE

fast, then found Deputy Leon Hatch's house and ruined his breakfast with the bad news.

The Wells Fargo office opened at eight o'clock. Colt was waiting at the door when the agent arrived for work. News of the sheriff's death and that of Hugo Hogan had spread fast. People were already milling on the streets talking about it. Also in the conversation was the fact that the tall, blond gunslinger had recovered a large portion of the money from the bank robberies.

The sleepy-eyed Fargo agent fumbled in his pocket for the door key. Setting his gaze on Dan Colt, he said, " 'Mornin'. C'n I help you, Mister Colt?"

"Little information."

"Okay," said the agent, turning the key.

"When do you expect Cadwell and Smythe through again?"

The agent's countenance clouded. Making a slight attempt at clearing his throat, he said, "Never."

Dan was not sure he had heard correctly. "What did you say, sir?"

"I said, *never*. Cadwell and Smythe, along with two passengers, were attacked by Comanches yesterday, ten miles south of Socorro. All killed."

Dan Colt could not believe his ears. This was like some kind of wild, unreal nightmare. Death had come like a hideous, stalking spectre and removed his every eyewitness. His only resource now was the affidavit.

Within an hour, the tall man had the bodies of the four deserters lashed to the saddles of their own horses. As he mounted the black, Leon Hatch said, "Don't you think it would be best to wait, Mister

Colt? Let the Indian trouble die down before you make the trip?"

"No time, Leon," replied Colt. "The longer I wait, the farther away my brother goes . . . and the closer Logan Tanner comes. Good luck."

"You're the one that's going to need that, Mister Colt," said Hatch. "Sure hope it all works out for you."

"Thanks," said Dan, spurring the gelding lightly.

Leon Hatch stood in the street and watched the four horses following Dan Colt until they passed from sight.

At eleven-thirty the next night, Dan rode into Socorro under cover of darkness. The whole town was asleep. He was bone-tired and he knew the horses were the same. They had had little rest since leaving Albuquerque. They needed feed and water. Dan was going to have to find a way to get the hostler's cooperation. He was still a criminal in the eyes of this town and there was no time for dispute.

Picking his way through the alleys in the moonlight, Dan headed for the livery stable. A big dog came off a back porch, barking furiously at the horses.

"Shut up, pooch!" Dan said in a hoarse whisper. The dog continued barking, nipping at the horses' heels. Dan was about to dismount and heave a rock at the hound, when one of the horses caught his nose with a swift kick. The dog yelped with pain and disappeared.

Pulling quietly into the yard behind the stable, Dan dismounted and rapped on the door of the hostler's living quarters. He waited a few seconds and rapped again. Presently a voice from inside acknowledged his presence. Half a minute later a lantern flared and the door came open. Squinting hard at the tall man, the hostler quickly recognized him. His eyes widened. He wheeled, lunging for a revolver that lay on a table.

With lightning speed, Dan palmed his right-hand .45 and eased back the hammer. The man checked his move.

"I don't have time to waste, mister," said Colt. "I've got some horses that need feed. I've got to tie you up. I'll feed them myself." Reaching in his vest pocket, he laid money on the table. "This will more than cover it."

Dan bound and gagged the hostler and led the horses into the barn. He relieved the four animals that bore the corpses by laying the corpses on the floor. Pouring grain in the manger and forking sufficient hay, he pumped water into the tank. He then climbed the ladder and stretched out in the hayloft.

The eastern horizon was showing a hint of gray light when the tall man awakened. Quietly, he slipped out of the barn and made his way through the gloom to the town's only hotel. There was a small lantern glowing in the lobby. No one was in sight. Tiptoeing to the desk he spun the register and ran his finger down the page. Checking the lobby another time, he softly mounted the stairs.

The corridor was dimly lit by low-burning lamps. Halting at room number four, Dan tapped lightly on the door. He waited a moment and was about to tap again when a soft feminine voice said, "Who is it?"

"Dan Colt," he half-whispered.

"Just a minute." Light footsteps went away, paused, then returned. The lock rattled and the door creaked open. Dan noted in the vague light that Marla was lovely, even when awakened from a sound sleep. She was clad in a long robe.

"Come in," she said, smiling. "I'll light the lantern."

"Better not," advised Dan, closing the door behind him. "I can only stay a minute. Don't dare arouse anyone." There was enough light filtering through the window that he could make out her face.

"Did you find your brother?" she asked, brushing at a wisp of hair that dangled on her forehead.

"I saw him, but he got away."

"Oh, Dan . . . I'm sorry."

"But I got the deserters, including the man who killed Ben Travers. They're all dead."

"Oh, thank God," she breathed. "I'm glad."

"But Dave still has your ring. I'm sorry."

"It's all right. Ben's killers have paid. That's the main thing. So now you're taking the bodies to the fort?"

"Yes. Got to get my hands on that affidavit."

Moving closer, Marla said, "The Comanches have been killing every white man in sight just south of here. Can't you wait till things are better?"

"No. Have to find Logan Tanner after I get the affidavit and go after Dave."

Moving closer yet, the beautiful Marla tilted her face upward. Her eyes clung desperately to the features of the rugged man who towered over her. A pungent warmth spread through his breast. Stirring within him was the same strange feeling she had caused before.

"Dan, when will I see you again?"

"I . . . I don't know. Where's home, Marla?"

"Denver."

"You're going back there now?"

"Yes. There's nothing for me here. I had to wait until I knew about you . . . and the killers."

"You have no family?"

"No. But I have a friend who owns a dress shop. I can make a living there." Her eyes looked deeply into his. "Will I see you again?"

"Maybe someday. After I find my brother. Clear myself with the law." Dan glanced at the growing light coming through the window. "I have to go," he said quietly.

Tears flooded Marla's eyes. Dan had to fight his arms to keep from reaching for her. Swallowing a hot lump, he said. "Good-bye, Marla. Maybe . . . maybe someday . . ."

Words were useless. The big man turned slowly, walked to the door and pulled it open. Looking at her tear stained face one more time, he stepped into the corridor and gently closed the door.

CHAPTER TWENTY-ONE

The rising sun mottled the fluent waters of the Rio Grande as Dan Colt led the four horses southward. Socorro slowly faded from view as the morning wore on. Dan took one last backward look as the cluster of buildings dissolved on the horizon. The warm memory of Marla Wells hung indelibly in his mind.

The tall man's gaze slowly probed the land around him. If the hate-crazed Comanches showed up, he would have to abandon the four corpses and ride for cover. The thought disturbed him. Without the bodies of Caraway, Deere, Stevens, and Hopper, Colonel Allen would not release the affidavit. Neither would there be any reward money. He was considerably more than halfway to the fort, now. It had taken three hours since leaving Socorro to reach this point. Another hour or so would bring him to the Colonel . . . and the precious document that would clear him with the law.

Dan wondered if Logan Tanner would be there waiting. He eagerly anticipated the look on the lawman's face when the cold, hard facts were presented to him.

An hour passed. Squinting and fixing his eyes on the southern horizon, he searched for the initial glimpse of the stockade wall that surrounded the fort. Nothing yet.

Dan took a few minutes to water the horses in the river, then returned to the trail. *Funny,* he thought peering southward, *should be able to see the wall by n—* Cold fingers squeezed his spine. Pulling rein, he stood up in the stirrups.

As Colt studied the formless black rubble, his heart sank within him. On the spot where the fort once stood were smoking heaps of charred wood. A few sections of adobe wall still stood to cast shadows over the ruins.

Dan slacked into the saddle, his face leaden. There was no movement anywhere. Had the Comanches wiped out everyone at the fort? Nudging the big black forward, he approached the ugly mass. Bodies of men, women, and children were scattered about. Some were burned beyond recognition. A few were still smoldering. Others were strewn outside the burned area.

A wave of nausea passed over the tall man. The air was heavy with the odor of burnt flesh and hair. Tears marred Dan Colt's vision. As he thumbed the watery film from his eyes, he caught sight of movement on the far side of the black rubble. It was a trooper. He was alive! The man was attempting to stand up.

Leaping from the saddle, Dan ran around the perimeter of the smoldering ruins. "Hey!" he shouted. "Trooper! I'm coming!"

The man looked up and sank back to the ground. As Dan rounded the far corner and drew near, his blood ran cold. The trooper's skin was black, he had been burned so severely. His hair was gone. His eyes looked like white pools in a bed of coal.

Kneeling beside him, Dan said, "Trooper..."

The man was breathing, but did not respond. He was lying knees-under-belly, face down. Attempting to ease him down to a more comfortable position, Dan grasped his shoulders. The charred uniform crackled softly and broke loose in his hands. He rolled the dying trooper onto his back.

"Trooper..." Dan said softly.

The man ran his tongue over his black lips and opened his eyes. Blinking painfully, he focused on Dan's face. Rolling his tongue, he said hoarsely, "Com—Comanches."

"Did anyone get away?" asked Colt anxiously.

"W-water..."

"Hang on," said Dan. "I'll be right back."

The heavy-hearted man ran to his horse, grabbed his canteen, and returned. With tender hands, he poured small amounts of water into the trooper's mouth. The man took a good portion and said, "Comanches."

"Did anyone get away?"

"No."

"The colonel? Colonel Allen?"

The trooper rolled his languid eyes. "Dead."

Dan Colt's pulse was throbbing in his temples and

the sides of his neck. "Trooper . . . can you hear me? Do you understand me?"

"Yes." His voice was growing weaker.

"Was there a U.S. marshal here within the last few days? Logan Tanner?"

The dying man swallowed hard. "Y-yes."

"Was he here when the attack came?"

"No. Left before . . . before . . ."

"I understand. Do you know if he was going north?"

"Was p-planning to . . . but . . . but Comanches w-wiped out stage . . . stagecoach just north . . . of here. Was going to . . . Las C-Cruces . . . instead."

Dan lifted his eyes to the smoldering remains of Fort Ryan. A bleak hopelessness came over him. Somewhere among those charred ruins were the ashes of the affidavit signed by Doctor George Springston. Gone was the documented proof that Dan Colt and Dave Sundeen were two different persons. He was back where he had started. Tanner would be dogging his tracks again.

Dropping his gaze to the trooper, he saw that the man was no longer breathing. The virulent hand of fate which had dealt Dan Colt such a savage blow had shown one kindness. The trooper had remained in this world long enough to spare him the torment of wondering whether Logan Tanner had seen the affidavit or not. Had he seen it, he would no doubt have waited at the fort for Dan's return.

Depositing the bodies of the deserters and the trooper in a common shallow grave, Dan turned the horses loose to fend for themselves and swung into the saddle. Pointing the gelding's nose northward, he rode away from the ruins of Fort Ryan. He would have to return to the spot where he had seen his twin. From there, he would pick up Dave's trail and continue his pursuit.

The sun was lowering on the western horizon, turning the desert a rosy red as Dan Colt guided the black across the Rio Grande and swung a wide berth around Socorro. Marla would be there until the stagecoaches were running regular again.

Stirring deep within the tall man was a desire to turn and ride into the town. But why develop a relationship? His life could never be normal until he found and captured Dave Sundeen. This had to be his only goal until it was done.

Casting one long, lingering look toward the town reddened by the sunset, he said within himself, *Maybe someday, Marla. Maybe someday the hand of fate will deal more kindly. Someday* ...

DELL'S ACTION-PACKED WESTERNS

Selected Titles

- [ ] **THE RELUCTANT PARTNER**
  by John Durham $1.50 (17770-7)
- [ ] **BOUGHT WITH A GUN** by Luke Short $1.50 (10744-5)
- [ ] **THE MAN FROM TUCSON**
  by Claude Cassady $1.50 (16940-2)
- [ ] **BOUNTY GUNS** by Luke Short $1.50 (10758-X)
- [ ] **DOUBLE-BARRELLED LAW**
  by D. L. Wrinkle $1.50 (11773-9)
- [ ] **THE KIOWA PLAINS** by Frank Ketchum $1.50 (14809-X)
- [ ] **LONG WAY TO TEXAS** by Lee McElroy $1.50 (14639-9)
- [ ] **LOCO** by Lee Hoffman $1.50 (14901-0)
- [ ] **LONG LIGHTNING** by Norman A. Fox $1.50 (14943-6)
- [ ] **DIL DIES HARD** by Kelly P. Gast $1.50 (12008-X)
- [ ] **BUCKSKIN MAN** by Tom W. Blackburn $1.50 (10976-0)
- [ ] **SHOWDOWN AT SNAKEGRASS JUNCTION**
  by Gary McCarthy $1.50 (18278-6)
- [ ] **SHORT GRASS** by Tom W. Blackburn $1.50 (17980-7)
- [ ] **DERBY MAN** by Gary McCarthy $1.50 (13297-5)
- [ ] **YANQUI** by Tom W. Blackburn $1.25 (19879-8)

At your local bookstore or use this handy coupon for ordering:

Dell **DELL BOOKS**
P.O. BOX 1000, PINEBROOK, N.J. 07058

Please send me the books I have checked above. I am enclosing $ _____
(please add 75¢ per copy to cover postage and handling). Send check or money order—no cash or C.O.D.'s. Please allow up to 8 weeks for shipment.

Mr/Mrs/Miss _____

Address _____

City _____ State/Zip _____

JOSEPH WAMBAUGH

author of *The Choirboys*

Joseph Wambaugh's "best novel yet!"
New York Daily News

Five Months on The New York Times Bestseller List

The Black Marble is Wambaugh's fifth bestseller and first love story! It tells the story of two unforgettable characters: Sgt. Valnikov, a damned good cop who turns far too frequently to the warmth and solace of Russian Vodka, and Natalie Zimmerman, an energetic woman detective determined to preserve the sanity and order of her division and to avoid at all costs the bad luck of the Black Marble. Together they fight crime, boredom, and each other and find more than they had ever hoped for!

A Dell Book $3.25 (10647-8)

At your local bookstore or use this handy coupon for ordering:

Dell	**DELL BOOKS** The Black Marble $3.25 (10647-8) **P.O. BOX 1000, PINEBROOK, N.J. 07058**

Please send me the above title. I am enclosing $_____
(please add 75¢ per copy to cover postage and handling). Send check or money order—no cash or C.O.D.'s. Please allow up to 8 weeks for shipment.

Mr/Mrs/Miss_____

Address_____

City_____ State/Zip_____

Another bestseller from the world's master storyteller

The Top of the Hill

IRWIN SHAW

author of *Rich Man, Poor Man* and *Beggarman, Thief*

He feared nothing...wanted everything. Every thrill. Every danger. Every woman.

"Pure entertainment. Full of excitement."—*N.Y. Daily News*

"You can taste the stale air in the office and the frostbite on your fingertips, smell the wood in his fireplace and the perfume scent behind his mistresses' ears."—*Houston Chronicle*

A Dell Book $2.95 (18976-4)

At your local bookstore or use this handy coupon for ordering:

| **Dell** | **DELL BOOKS** THE TOP OF THE HILL $2.95 (18976-4)
P.O. BOX 1000, PINEBROOK, N.J. 07058 |

Please send me the above title. I am enclosing $_____
(please add 75¢ per copy to cover postage and handling). Send check or money order—no cash or C.O.D.'s. Please allow up to 8 weeks for shipment.

Mr/Mrs/Miss _____

Address _____

City _____ State/Zip _____

SOLO

by JACK HIGGINS

author of The Eagle Has Landed

The pursuit of a brilliant concert pianist/master assassin brings this racing thriller to a shattering climax in compelling Higgins' fashion.

A Dell Book $2.95   (18165-8)

At your local bookstore or use this handy coupon for ordering.

Dell	**DELL BOOKS** SOLO $2.95 (18165-8) P.O. BOX 1000, PINEBROOK, N.J. 07058

Please send me the above title. I am enclosing $_____
(please add 75¢ per copy to cover postage and handling). Send check or money order—no cash or C.O.D.'s. Please allow up to 8 weeks for shipment.

Mr/Mrs/Miss_____

Address_____

City_____ State/Zip_____

**A true odyssey of love and evil
by the author of Blood and Money**

SERPENTINE

by Thomas Thompson

A chilling factual account of exotically handsome, demonically charming mass-murder, Charles Sobhraj. "Shocking impact...marks Thompson as one of the finest nonfiction writers of the decade."—Philadelphia Inquirer

"The most bizarre true-crime narrative since the Manson story Helter Skelter...Grotesque, baffling, and hypnotic."—San Francisco Chronicle

A Dell Book $3.50   (17611-5)

At your local bookstore or use this handy coupon for ordering:

| Dell | DELL BOOKS   SERPENTINE $3.50   (17611-5)
P.O. BOX 1000, PINEBROOK, N.J. 07058 |

Please send me the above title. I am enclosing $ _____
(please add 75¢ per copy to cover postage and handling). Send check or money order—no cash or C.O.D.'s. Please allow up to 8 weeks for shipment.

Mr/Mrs/Miss _____

Address _____

City _____ State/Zip _____

 **Bestsellers**

- [ ] **THE RING** by Danielle Steel $3.50 (17386-8)
- [ ] **INGRID BERGMAN: MY STORY**
  by Ingrid Bergman and Alan Burgess $3.95 (14085-4)
- [ ] **SOLO** by Jack Higgins $2.95 (18165-8)
- [ ] **THY NEIGHBOR'S WIFE** by Gay Talese....$3.95 (18689-7)
- [ ] **THE CRADLE WILL FALL** by Mary H. Clark $3.50 (11476-4)
- [ ] **RANDOM WINDS** by Belva Plain $3.50 (17158-X)
- [ ] **WHEN THE WIND BLOWS** by John Saul $3.50 (19857-7)
- [ ] **LITTLE GLORIA ... HAPPY AT LAST**
  by Barbara Goldsmith $3.50 (15109-0)
- [ ] **CHANGE OF HEART** by Sally Mandel $2.95 (11355-5)
- [ ] **THE PROMISE** by Danielle Steel $3.50 (17079-6)
- [ ] **FLOWERS OF THE FIELD**
  by Sarah Harrison $3.95 (12584-7)
- [ ] **LOVING** by Danielle Steel $3.50 (14657-7)
- [ ] **CORNISH HEIRESS** by Roberta Gellis $3.50 (11515-9)
- [ ] **BLOOD RED WINE** by Laurence Delaney....$2.95 (10714-8)
- [ ] **COURT OF THE FLOWERING PEACH**
  by Janette Radcliffe $3.50 (11497-7)
- [ ] **FAIR WARNING**
  by George Simpson and Neal Burger $3.50 (12478-6)

At your local bookstore or use this handy coupon for ordering:

Dell **DELL BOOKS**
P.O. BOX 1000, PINEBROOK, N.J. 07058

Please send me the books I have checked above. I am enclosing $ _____
(please add 75¢ per copy to cover postage and handling). Send check or money
order—no cash or C.O.D.'s. Please allow up to 8 weeks for shipment.

Mr/Mrs/Miss _____

Address _____

City _____ State/Zip _____